# TRAPPED BY THE FAE

## ZORA FOX

## ❧ I ❧

I thought that seeing the Other Kingdom of the Fae would be different.

I knew all about the dangers, of course. Nobody in Selene would stop talking about the dangers. Even my sister Laura cautioned me about walking near the woods at night. It was nothing but hourly warnings.

Why couldn't I be free?

The appeal of goblin men and forest creatures and alluring Fae nagged at my imagination. Despite having offers to settle down with children in Selene, that life wasn't something I wanted. Only when I realized that marrying could help those I loved most did I even consider it. Consistent food and warmth were strong motivators.

Grandmother hated that men didn't need to fear about any of it as the women did unless they did something stupid like plunging into the forest to confront the Fae King. I agreed with her. But, while Grandmother hated men, I rather liked them. Just not enough to let one dictate my life.

Little did I know that the Fae King would marry my careful sister Laura. I, on the other hand, would get stuck on this side of the barrier, on the Fae side, with no gorgeous, powerful lover, only a craving I couldn't shake.

I longed for fairy fruit.

No, that wasn't the right word. If there was a stronger one, Laura would know it.

I yearned for it. I obsessed about it. Fairy fruit cycled like a maddening song every day. I wanted to suck its juices, feel the sweet poison of its bliss...

But my prison guards, as I dubbed them, offered us none.

Every day they swept into the East Wing where all the maidens from Selene for generations past lived together since waking from their sleep. We had all at some time heeded the call to taste the fruit. I was the last victim so I still had some of my youth but the rest were mostly husks of once vivacious women. Honestly, I hated being lumped together with them. They made me feel dead, and we reinforced each other's craving for the fruit, since all of us had that in common.

So when we saw the leather-clad Fae enter our quarters, we swarmed for some of their life and the faint possibility that this time—*this time*—they would finally bring what we yearned for.

But fairy fruit would speed our decomposition, they said, particularly one.

Calyse was the Fae King's friend or helper or something. Honestly, I didn't care.

I didn't care that he was unfairly handsome, far outstripping any boy I'd snogged in Selene.

I didn't care that he delivered his bad news with a smile.

I didn't care that he made a point to seek me out among the hateful sea of white gowns because I was Laura's sister.

He represented my situation, the hopeless cycle binding me to this place. Fairy fruit had cursed me to life on this side of the barrier, never to return to the human world, and it was my only solace. Calyse, for all his consideration, didn't give me the one thing that could help me.

On nights when I was lucid enough to think as I lay there in my little marble bedroom, I felt that my life had ended.

❧

I DIDN'T NEED TO BE TAKEN CARE OF. I NEEDED FAIRY FRUIT and freedom.

I sat at a large table in the center of the space that had been converted into a compound for the women. Glittering bits like stars shone overhead in the deep blue ceiling. Semi-transparent whisps of cloth fluttered ghostlike just beyond the edge of properly seeing. The walls too were more magnificent than anything back home in Selene, covered with paintings done directly over the black marble. Male and female figures with beautiful bodies walked or danced or coupled in the woods. Normally, the scandalous artwork would have delighted me, but I had little capacity for delight this morning.

Surrounded by the other pale, white-clad women, as well as several beautiful Fae attendants bringing in new dishes, I felt only a simmering despair. Grapes and buttery pastry and thick soup with butternut squash and fried bacon sat in front of me. I knew it was wrong not to enjoy it, but flavors had dulled after that night of poisonous abandon in the forest.

The woman next to me, five years my senior, nibbled at the crust. I knew she had the same thoughts.

"Not hungry?" came a jovial voice behind me.

I released a breath before turning around. Calyse always singled me out, and it hadn't made me popular among our sad little group.

He stood there by the end of the bench, smiling. Today, he wore the thick strands of his black hair up in a knotted bun at the back of his head. Leathers that accentuated his generous muscles covered his body neck to ankle. His armor, his hair, and even his skin were all dark, except his eyes, which flamed orange with merriment.

"Not very," I replied.

"She's talking, though," he said.

It had taken me three weeks before I could speak lucidly. If I was honest with myself, I felt ashamed and angry that my recovery from the enchanted sleep was taking this long.

"The Queen wants you to visit the training ground today," he went on, "if you're finished with your meal." He gave a pointed look at my full plate.

I was no longer as emaciated and weak as I had been, so I didn't see that it was his business if I had an appetite or not. I lowered my voice so the other women were less likely to hear. "Did you bring me anything *else* to eat?"

"You know I can't," he said, mouth tipping to the side apologetically.

The women next to me raised her head, suddenly attuned to our conversation.

I spoke even more quietly. "What can I do for you in exchange?" I drew a finger down his forearm. Calyse's warrior build and ruggedly gorgeous features made flirting easy, even though he aggravated me to no end. Perhaps today he would finally heed my request.

He took my hand gently but firmly and placed it on the

wooden tabletop. "That would be great, I'm sure, but I still won't disobey the King and Queen. Besides," he said, getting louder, "you want to live a full, happy life of brooding, don't you?"

I clenched my teeth. "I'm finished," I said. "We can go to the training ground."

I did want to see more of the castle. It was as though more than one Lizzie lived inside me. One still loved adventure and flirting and wanted to see more of the world. The other wanted to curl in on itself, devouring fairy fruit until I had my fill and my life snuffed out around it. The clash between the two ground me down until I felt like an open wound.

I rose from the table and followed Calyse's broad form out of the enormous, nightlit dining area.

"It's where I was going anyway," he said.

I didn't respond.

We strode down long passageways and rooms as cavernous as mountains and ornate doors carved with metal beasts. Regal Fae and sleek predatory creatures on leashes passed us, beautiful beings with sensually mussed countenances, and then... My heart skipped. A male forest creature. He had the features and coloring of a fox, but mixed with human intelligence and movement. I gazed after him when he passed, his tawny tail flowing behind him. Forest creatures knew where the fairy fruit was. They'd offered it to me the first time. Together we'd drunk the sticky-sweet juice and eaten ice-cold melon and fallen into a mindless bliss of sensation.

I swallowed against my prickly throat and continued.

The walk to the training ground was long, as long as it would have taken to stroll from one end of Selene to the other. This castle where Fae held me captive felt as big as a planet.

Finally, the two of us emerged into a room that struck me as what the inside of an autumn stump would look like if it were expanded a thousand times. The walls were wooden with thick natural grooves running vertically up the walls. Within the grooves were weapons and armor and sashes and cushions and anything else one needed to practice fighting. Platforms arched out like a chaos of mushrooms, complete with gills beneath.

My sister Laura stood on one of them far above us, hands outstretched. Her husband, the Fae King Endymion, stood behind her. Even from my position, I could see a self-satisfied smirk on his face as he watched Laura, magnificent in a leather and blue gown, shoot smoke-like shadows from her hands in a thick stream.

I shoved down a twinge of jealousy. Laura had chosen her fate, and I was proud of her for it. She understood her place here in the Other Kingdom. I floated as aimless as dust on the wind.

"Laura! End!" Calyse shouted, waving.

The couple looked down. Laura beamed at me. She had golden eyes now that matched the King's and, I was told, mine as well. But she was my Laura, no longer frightened but strong and brave and well-loved. I smiled back.

Calyse led me to the cunning little staircase leading up to the top of the mushroom platform where she stood. He embraced the King, also wickedly handsome with dark hair, bronze skin, a sultry mouth, and golden cuffs on his ears. All the Fae invited temptation, as the legends of my childhood had proclaimed. I wasn't surprised that Laura finally fancied this one.

"Lizzie!" Laura gave me a hug. "I'm glad you were well enough to come."

"You think I would miss seeing you in a Fae combat training ground?" I teased.

"I'm trying to figure out more about what I can do with these shadows," she explained, holding out a palm where a seething mass of darkness flickered. She made a fist. The shadows puffed into nothing.

I didn't have any expertise or guess to add, so I simply said, "What can you do now?"

She blushed, the faintest bit of the old Laura coming through.

"Terrible things," Endymion interjected in his low voice. His tone didn't suggest that he disliked whatever it was she could do.

"I enjoy this one," Laura said, stepping to the edge of the platform, planting one foot back, and blasting two streams of darkness from her palms. She hit a collection of domed helmets, which scattered madly across the floor.

I gave a little laugh. "I never would have guessed this future for you when we were children," I said, laying a hand on her shoulder and speaking into her ear, "when you hurried home so dutifully when the sun started going down. *We must not look at goblin men,*" I sang, although my voice was croaky. "Who knew they'd look like *that*?"

Already, fatigue was settling in my bones, but I didn't want Laura to know. She looked so happy. There was no reason to draw her into a misery that should be mine alone.

"And you!" I continued. "That gown." I raised my eyebrows.

"I know," she said, unconsciously tracing the leather cutouts at her waist, "I never would have worn this at home, but I like it now." She scrutinized me with her cat-like gaze. Did she see my craving, my dissatisfaction beneath? "We should have sent new gowns to all the maidens before this," she told Endymion over my head.

"Am I the dress deliverer now?" Calyse chimed in. His tone was light, but I hated it anyway.

"There's no need," I found myself saying, even though Fae gowns sounded heavenly.

"I'll send them right away," Laura said.

I tried to look properly grateful. I loved my sister more than life, but it hurt to see her almost as much as it hurt not to see her. The two Lizzies. "Thank you," I managed, and squeezed her sideways.

But I didn't need to be taken care of. I needed fairy fruit and freedom.

$\maltese$   2   $\maltese$

I asked a Fae attendant for a mirror. For a castle full of stunningly attractive creatures, there seemed to be no mirrors at all.

Laura had followed through with her promise to send gowns for all the women in the East Wing and had even visited me herself to narrow down my favorites. I kissed her when she left.

Now, this was the first time I'd seen myself in months. My blonde hair had grown longer, my face and arms thinner, my skin paler. My eyes shone hungry like a feral cat's. In Selene, those eyes had harbored hope, but all I saw now was fiery craving. I looked away.

The only element I truly enjoyed seeing was the dress, grass green and shiny. The skirt flowed like water whenever I moved. A brocade of tiny golden flowers encircled my waist, pinching tightly to accentuate the swell of my breasts and hips. These days, I was less shapely than I had been in the village, but this dress made me feel as though I could perhaps find my way back to those days when I was desirable.

I was capable then, too.

I stood in the middle of my room, like a jeweled marble tomb, and crossed my arms. I was capable now, although not in as many ways. If I wanted freedom or fairy fruit, I could go out and find them.

"You look conspiratorial."

I whirled. Calyse stood in the doorway, sweaty from his time in the training grounds. He had stayed when I returned to the East Wing. That had been hours ago.

He fixed me with a look, one eyebrow popping up as though he knew what I was thinking.

"I'm never conspiratorial."

"I'd wager my tongue that you were at one time."

"You don't have to be here," I said, uncrossing my arms. "Surely, you have better things to do than babysit a grown woman?" When I'd awoken, I discovered that I had missed my twenty-first birthday to fairy fruit-induced sleep.

"To be honest, the King doesn't need me as much as he used to, so I have more time to make sure you're doing all right. Besides, I have more time in general. I could lose a year looking after you and not miss it. I know you love it so when I pop in."

I blinked slowly, hoping he caught onto my disgust. "Thank you," I said slowly, "for helping my sister, but I'm all right now. I know I... wasn't... for a while, but I can look after myself, and you can tell her that."

"Your body has nearly returned to normal," he agreed. Behind his statement, though, he disagreed that I was all right.

"As though you would know."

"I saw you when you arrived."

"And you were looking that closely?"

"I didn't need to be looking closely, but I'll say I was if it will make you happy." His sweaty face turned mischievous.

My pulse jumped, which only made me angrier. I noticed that

about the Fae. They were quick—quick to appear, quick to anger, quick to laugh, and quick to flirt. It didn't mean anything. Laura and Endymion had certainly been quick to fall in love.

In Selene, if a boy flirted with me, I could assume that they wanted a relationship. Sometimes, to my detriment, I simply liked flirting. I'd received four proposals before ending up across the barrier. Here, these beautiful beings were so naturally seductive that I couldn't tell what they wanted out of flirting with one another. Well, I could tell... But I didn't know if that meant they wanted the commitment of a relationship to go with the pleasurable encounter.

"What would make me happy is if you brought me what I asked for," I said archly. "You wouldn't need to bring much, just a taste."

His face fell. His golden-orange gaze dropped and a line formed between his brows. Calyse was normally so glib. Did this mean he was considering it?

My heart beat faster.

When he met my eyes again, he'd clearly made a decision. My skin tingled in anticipation. I tried to keep my breathing even.

He exhaled. "You're stuck in here all the time just... thinking. That can't be good for anybody. I think you need a distraction."

I deflated. "A distraction?"

"Something to take your mind off fairy fruit."

As disappointed as I was, I had to admit I was a little curious. The world of the Fae had only flashed by in disjointed pieces. For a while I swayed between reality and dreams, so half of what I saw might not even have been real.

Fairy fruit and freedom. What if this could give me the latter?

Calyse went on. "There are many, many things to experience in this castle if you know where to go. I haven't experienced most of them either, at least not since the Great Sleep, but I know where they are. Different pleasures. You can lose yourself in a way that doesn't cause your body to age and decay and die." He grimaced good-naturedly.

I narrowed my eyes at him. He didn't know what he was talking about, but his talk of different pleasures piqued my interest. I almost asked if it was safe to go, but realized how much I sounded like Laura had back in Selene and decided I didn't care whether it was or not. If Calyse suggested something, no doubt it would be safe for me, even though I was a mortal.

"What pleasures?" I asked. "I'm interested."

"And you no longer look like a dollop of snow on a branch, which is helpful."

"*You*, however, look sweaty and disgusting." I closed my mouth. The first was true but the second unfair. And untrue. Calyse looked muscled as a statue under those leathers and his face would have drawn me the second I saw it in the village. But we weren't in the village anymore. Everyone was like that, and he didn't deserve all my snappishness. My temper didn't used to be this short. "I'm sorry. It's true, but I'm sorry. So, what are you suggesting?"

He bit back a laugh. His strong jaw worked for a moment before he continued. "It depends on what would distract you most effectively. I play the flute, for example."

He guffawed at my pained reaction. "No? Another time then. The King doesn't like it either, but he has no ear for music. Hmm." He chewed the corner of his full lip. "There are parties— drinking, dancing. Ever since your sister defeated Im Scathail, they've doubled, not that I've been to many recently. Like I said, I've been busy."

"Dancing?" My little glimmer of excitement grew brighter.

A grin spread over his face. "Are you sure your delicate human sensibilities can handle it?"

"Handle dancing? I'm a good dancer," I said indignantly. "Where do I go?"

"A Fae dance," he clarified. "I've never been to a human one but they sound boring by comparison. Ours can last days. You probably don't want to enter on the final day. Most of the clothes and the wine will be gone by then."

My lips fell open. I couldn't tell if he was kidding. If he was, then it wouldn't be the first time. He seemed to draw pleasure from trying to scandalize me. Little did he know that, compared to the other women in the East Wing, at least, I was hard to scandalize. I drew myself up. "You didn't say where it was."

❧

As far as I could tell, it was only afternoon, though time moved differently in the Other Kingdom. Despite the early hour, a party was already in full swing in a room on the little visited third floor.

Caramel and spun sugar and musk and something spicy to balance the sweetness floated through the air. I smiled. The small room—by Fae standards—was full. I noticed that there were no forest creatures here, although I often saw them in other areas of the castle. Here, it was only Fae. The males and females all called to something deep inside me with their immaculate beauty. They danced like something choreographed, like something wild, like something that could make me forget.

The room was stone, not marble, like a cave. Tables abundant with wine and food dotted the entire space. Of course, I scanned for fairy fruit. Some succulent fruit piled high on the tables, but none of them tugged at the pit of my stomach like fairy fruit would.

I glanced up at Calyse. "This happens all the time?"

"Are you surprised?" he asked. Something in his face looked fascinated too, though.

I stepped forward among the moving bodies of the Fae. I'd never felt insufficient before, but even with my new gown, I remembered how skinny I looked, with dark circles around my eyes. Yes, I'd gained back lucidity, but that wasn't much in the face of these magnificent beings.

Summoning boldness, I slid between them. The music of drums and flutes and whirling strings flowed around me.

Some eyed me with haughtiness and others with open curiosity. I avoided the haughty ones and approached a young-looking male with glowing eyes, mottled blue and gold. I'd never seen such a combination. He had short, curly brown hair, light skin (though not as pale as mine), and a lithe body, arms and lips made for sin. He wore an open drawstring shirt of dark green and tight fawn-colored trousers. He regarded me openly with his lidded eyes.

Someone bumped into me as they danced, a slight spray of drink spray speckling me. A strong hand held me steady, though I'd already righted myself.

A dimple appeared in the mottle-eyed Fae's cheek. "You're new, little human," he said.

It was on my lips to claim Laura—their queen—as my sister, but I bit back the statement. I wanted to make my own way here, not be treated differently because people knew that I was related to royalty or that I had been put in enchanted sleep. Let them wonder why I was here. If they couldn't put those things together themselves, I wouldn't tell them.

"Yes, I've never been to one of these parties before," I said, wrapping the drawstring of his shirt around my finger. This Fae didn't seem to be with anyone, and he seemed pleased enough to talk to me.

A distraction. Calyse was right. My mind skipped less frantically to my craving now. I was in the kingdom of the Fae, where all was luxury and pleasure and passion. There was no one to scold me if I indulged myself.

"No?" He drew out the word in a tipsy, suggestive way, wrapping his free hand firmly around my waist. Even the boys in the village, eager for a tumble, hid their desires a little. This Fae did not.

"Initiate me," I said, feeling rather drunk myself. I leaned my meager weight against him and rubbed my thumb against the corner of his lips as though wiping something off.

This gathering reminded me of the woodland hollow I encountered when I first tried fairy fruit. The forest creatures, so varied, so strange, so beautiful, had all lounged together, partaken together. I had lost myself to them. The memory hypnotized me.

The Fae and I ground together in a dance that left me wet with longing.

Longing.

The craving.

"Do you have," I panted, feeling the strong muscles of the Fae undulating against me, "fairy fruit here?"

"I don't think so."

I swallowed, stroked the warm hair at his nape. "Where could I find some?"

"We have more..." He faded.

What did he mean? "More what?"

We had moved toward the wall. He kissed me and stopped our scandalous dance. When he pulled away, I watched him in confusion as he reached around a couple and plucked something off a table.

It couldn't be...? I snatched it from him. A plum cake. Frustration lanced through me, not only at the revelation that there was no fairy fruit here, but at my own fixation that wouldn't let me think of anything else.

The Fae bent to kiss me again, but I frowned and dodged the advance. This wouldn't do.

I had thought Calyse was right but, as usual, he didn't understand what I needed or how broken I was.

❀   3   ❀

"Little mortal," cooed a female voice. I looked into the eyes of a curvy, auburn-haired beauty. She too had stepped away from the dancing. Even after weeks in the castle, I hadn't gotten used to the variety of stunning people here. They seemed to have walked out of one of Laura's fairy stories. "I know where to find fairy fruit."

The handsome Fae forgotten, I caught my breath. "Where?"

Could it be this easy after all? No wonder Calyse and the attendants usually prevented us from leaving the East Wing. It was for our own good, they said.

Fuck that.

"The kitchens," she said simply. "It is delicious." The next words she spoke into my ear, "But I think it harms little humans like you. It's too much." She straightened, teasing.

I tried to hide my excitement. "I'd love to try some."

She placed a long finger against her full mouth. "Shall I steal you, though?"

I glanced behind me. The mottle-eyed Fae was gone. I didn't

have the opportunity to regret him. This Fae woman could lead me to fairy fruit.

"Steal me, please," I said.

Her laughter was rich as wine. "Come on."

Only then did I realize she held an exotic bird by a tether with her other arm. Pet and owner matched.

We wove together through the crowd to the far wall. Happily we didn't have to pass the entrance I'd used. What if Calyse were still there? He did like to stay where he wasn't wanted.

The music and the dancing bodies and the scent of food faded behind us. She led me down new back ways. Dimly, I noticed architectural and artistic wonders, but couldn't give them any attention. My limbs had new strength.

"What is your name?" she asked.

"Elizabeth of Selene."

"Selene? Now, that is interesting. Our new victorious queen— long live Her Majesty—comes from Selene." Both she and the red bird looked at me. "You also have blonde hair."

A pull behind my sternum said something wasn't right. "So do many people there."

"But many people do not visit Tylaith Castle."

"I'm more adventurous than most."

"I see that," she purred, stroking the bird's feathers.

My heart beat hard in my chest, not only for the promise of satisfying my craving but because of something else I couldn't place. I followed the Fae deeper down the halls. The metal sconces became dimmer. "Are the kitchens nearby?" I asked, fully aware that the kitchens could be still far off, given the apparent size of this place.

"Not far," she said, slowing so she could link her free arm through mine. "The fruit you ask for, it is decadent."

I suddenly didn't want her for a confidante. "You could simply... point me in the right direction, then."

"If you wish," she said, unlooping her arm. The bird pecked at her hair and gave a little chirp. Her tone held no malice, but I felt relieved when she let go. Raising an elegant arm, she pointed to a lighted doorway just up ahead. "Through there. You'll find all the fairy fruit you could desire, but don't devour it at once. Humans pay a—"

I was already at the door, pulling open the sculpted metal handle, when it struck me.

The Fae woman's eyes had been completely black.

I shuddered, but my skin still tingled with excitement. Fae and forest creatures within the hot room stirred pots, climbed ladders, chopped ingredients. They noticed me, but didn't prevent me from entering.

Where was it? So many smells mingled in the air that I couldn't differentiate the one I needed. Huge bunches of herbs, animal carcasses, heaps of vegetables, jars of honey...

My need had spiked so high I felt about to burst from my own skin. Breathless, I finally approached the nearest forest creature, an antlered male with shining brown eyes.

"I have been given orders to dispose of all fairy fruit in this kitchen. Can you show me where it is so I can take it away?"

Suspicion permeated his look.

"I'm Lizzie, Laura's sister. Of Selene. It's her order, the Queen's order, that it all be removed."

After a pregnant pause, someone confirmed, "It is her sister."

Almost dizzy with relief, I nodded. "It needs to be taken out tonight."

The forest creature pivoted slowly, like an animal trying not to be heard, and walked slowly and reached slowly into a pantry. I nearly screamed with impatience.

Down-cheeked peaches and pomegranates full and fine, rare pears, figs to fill my mouth... The basket he drew out had them all.

Before I could take the handle from him, I'd already thrust figs into my mouth while my fingers bled with red pomegranate juice when I ripped one open. The taste was an instant relief. It was ecstasy; it was all things good and bad that I wanted; it was home.

"Wait," someone said.

I crushed a peach in my hand, sweet and sticky against my fingers and my lips.

The forest creature flinched away. I reached for the basket handle, laughing at the game. Missing it, I grabbed a cluster of grapes instead.

I was short of breath. My vision blurred.

I needed more.

I needed more...

❦

WATER SPLASHED ON MY FACE. I SAT UP, COUGHING AND spluttering. The water in my mouth tasted like the dregs of fairy fruit. Once I collected myself, I licked my lips and looked up.

I sat on the ground in the kitchen. Above me were Laura, wrapped in a robe, and King Endymion. The antlered boy held an empty bucket beside them. The basket of fairy fruit was nowhere to be seen. My throat closed.

Laura's golden eyes glistened with tears. "Lizzie..." It was clearly the beginning of a question, but none materialized.

"Laura..." Mine was the beginning of an excuse or promise, but I couldn't lie to her.

Endymion glared, piercing and a little disgusted, then addressed the kitchen staff. "Destroy all fairy fruit in Tylaith Castle. It's too dangerous for humans."

"No!" My desperation was too great to censor myself. "No, please, I'll do better. I won't seek it out until I can control myself."

The King ignored me. "Every piece. And on the grounds."

I stood. Although I was taller than Laura, the King still towered above me. What did he matter to me anyway? Laura would understand. I took her hand in mine, only to realize how sticky mine was. "Laura, please. You almost tasted it. Do you have any idea...?" But I didn't know how to proceed.

"I love you, Lizzie," she replied evenly, "so much. You can hardly know how much. But this is for the best."

I swatted her hands away. Before I could return mine to my sides, Endymion had caught the offending palm in his rough fingers, squeezing until it hurt. I didn't flinch.

"No one hurts my bride. Not even you," he growled, and dropped my hand.

"I didn't hurt you, did I?" I asked.

"No, she didn't hurt me."

Endymion huffed. The light in the kitchen sparkled on the golden ear cuff he wore.

"I didn't mean to hurt you, but you can't mean that," I said, trying to catch her full attention.

She gazed back at me. For a moment, there were only the two of us, both trapped here, but now she was happy and I was... Anger rose up in me again but I did my best to temper it down.

"You're not well," she whispered.

"You have no right to say so," I snapped. "If I want to ruin myself, just let me. I have no other purpose here."

I hadn't even felt the sting of tears pressing against my eyes before I was sobbing against her shoulder. I held her tight like a drowning woman needs driftwood.

❅   4   ❅

Istayed in bed all the next day and the next. I didn't eat. I screamed into my pillow when the pent-up craving for fairy fruit became too much.

The knowledge that now I couldn't reach it, maybe could never reach it, ate at me like disease. My skin felt papery and my eyes burned, though no more tears fell.

"Your sister's concerned about you," said a low, light-hearted voice.

My gaze shot to the door. "Knock, won't you?"

It was Calyse. Of course. It was foolish to think he wouldn't intrude on my rest. He leaned insolently against the doorjamb. "Believe it or not, checking up on you is not always my favorite activity either. I want to know you're all right as much as the King and Queen do, but you're snappy as a dog." He heaved a deep breath into his broad chest. "I've been ordered to keep a closer eye on you, make sure you eat and don't go anywhere alone."

My mouth opened.

He held up his dark hands to prevent my raging response. He

had a large raised scar across one palm. "I can't disobey a direct order, even when a lovely girl hates it."

"Isn't that what you've already been doing?" I asked in despair.

"No, just the occasional check up. Now…" He sighed, the first hint of actual consternation entering his expression. "It appears to be a full-time job."

My brows clashed together. Lip curling, I tried to form a response, but nothing came out. This level of surveillance was…

"For how long?" I demanded, hurt that Laura, of all people, understood me so little. The question was all that my thoughts could form coherently.

He shrugged a big shoulder. Shouldn't he care? He was stuck doing something he didn't want either. "Until you're well enough," they said.

"What does that mean?"

"I'm not a doctor or a medium. I have no way of telling. So let's try to make the best of it."

I took a tiny bit of pride in the way I'd finally managed to irk him. Calyse, who was so maddeningly unflappable.

"Are you going to stay here all day, then?" he asked.

I snuggled back down into the black silk sheets of my bed. It was a stark contrast to the mostly white marble walls. "Yes."

"In that case, I'll bring you some food."

"Wait—"

But he had shut the door.

Minutes later, Calyse, not an attendant, brought a huge slab of steak on a tray. Smaller assorted dishes held salads and creams, but I couldn't get past the portion of meat. The sheet stretched as he set the tray upon little stands on either side of my thighs.

"Really?" I asked, laughing. "Am I a pack of wolves?"

"You don't like it?"

I still had no appetite, but I took up the golden silverware and started sawing off a human-sized bite from the enormous steak. "It would take me three days to eat this." To make my point, I demonstrated the small amount at the end of my fork before stuffing it pointedly into my mouth.

"This is not my normal occupation, if you haven't noticed," he said, having a harder time than usual reaching for lightness.

"What is your normal occupation?" The steak was actually quite good, better than anything I'd eaten in Selene. The reminder sobered me again. That was a home I could never return to.

"I'm part of the King's guard," he said.

"Now you're part of my guard." I fished around in one of the salads. "How does it feel to be demoted?"

"It's not a demotion at all. The temporary bodyguard—"

"Babysitter."

"—of the Queen's sister? The one she loves most besides the King? It's an honor." A thoughtful dimple appeared in his cheek. "I've been asked to do far worse things." He summoned a smile when he looked back up into my eyes.

The pause stretched.

And stretched.

"If I stay here all day," I said, "does that mean you stay here too?"

"I could step outside the door."

I groaned.

"I could also get closer if you prefer," he said with a wink.

"Only if you want half this steak," I said, eyebrows raised at the offending dish. If he was disappointed that I didn't take his bait, he didn't show it.

"I'll step outside," he said. "May you sleep short and live long." He pressed a fist to his chest in a sort of salute before leaving.

I exhaled in relief to be alone again.

But then I realized that I hadn't thought about fairy fruit during my entire interaction with Calyse. In an odd way, nettling him gave me some reprieve from my constant longing. Perhaps Laura did know what she was doing.

"If I have to carry you out of here, I will. There is an infinite number of more interesting things to do than lingering and doing nothing."

"Is that what you tell the King?"

"I don't have to. He lets me train or leave or play the flute until he needs me. And he's interesting."

"I'm not?"

I lay in bed for the sixth day in a row. The aftereffect of fairy fruit had left me listless and fatigued, though I was admittedly strong enough to leave the room.

"Not at the moment." He picked idly at his scar, leaning against my doorpost on one muscle-thickened arm. He left his hair down today, the twisted strands fanning out like a sunburst from his forehead and falling to his shoulders.

"I thought you were kidding about the flute," I said.

He met my eyes mischievously. "Why does everybody assume I'm joking about that? Everyone has interests."

I flexed my jaw, hesitating. "I'm sorry you have to watch me. I would dismiss you if I could."

"Ah," he said knowingly, "there's the problem. Shall we go out?"

To tell the truth, I was getting bored myself, and I did have enough energy to do more than lounge in bed. Myself from a year ago would have been appalled to look at me. I had such hopes then. Even bookbinding seemed like an adventure. Any time I could travel to the neighboring town to sell a book, I felt a thrill of independence.

This Lizzie was letting Laura down.

"Yes," I replied, rising and gathering an outfit besides the dirty white one I wore. "Let's go out."

"No more slipping away at parties," he said, obviously pleased to be doing something other than guarding the door.

"You'll simply have to stay close," I teased.

"Very close," he countered.

I cheated a look at him. I could never tell if his flirtations were genuine, since he seemed to speak that way with everyone. A naughty smile quirked his lips.

He surrendered to a bark of laughter. "Where do you want to go, Lizzie?"

"To lose myself," I said before thinking about it.

"I know just the thing."

❧

I DIDN'T EXPECT TO END UP BACK IN THE TRAINING AREA. AS before, it was all but abandoned. Were there no more threats, no battles left to fight? It seemed strange.

I gave Calyse a curious look. "I thought you'd show me a new part of the castle or something. Perhaps take me to a ritual where they drink blood."

His eyes widened in surprise. Perhaps he hadn't expected me

to talk like that. "No blood, no," he said, a grin widening his face. "At least, not if you do as I say."

A bolt of apprehension shot through me. We stood in the shade of one of the enormous mushroom-platforms.

He approached me, close enough to encase most of my arm in his meaty hand. His skin smelled faintly of amber and smoke. "This won't do." He let me go, and the sudden lack of pressure, of contact, wasn't a relief.

Wooden staves lined one crevice of the wall. He stalked toward them, sturdy and sure, and grabbed two.

When he was still a fair way off, he threw one to me. I flailed both hands in front of my face and managed to catch it.

"I come here when I need to forget about something," he said. "If the body's working hard enough, it's all you can focus on. So" —he bent his knees and stared a challenge at me—"try to hit me. I can see I annoy you. You have anger. Let it out." The amused tilt of his lips suggested it would be humorous to watch me try.

I ground my teeth, though I had to admit he had concocted a pretty satisfying plan. I gripped the stave, feeling the wood grain against my fingers. He held his in one hand over and behind his head.

For a moment I scanned for a weak spot. I was no warrior, not in this sense, but I could hit him. I was sure of it.

His orange eyes glinted at me, far too pleased at my hesitation.

I slid one foot forward just to see what he would do.

Nothing.

I slid it further, adjusting my handle on the stave.

Still, he didn't move, just teased me with that look.

Finally, I struck, whipping the stave sideways to strike him in the arm that didn't hold a weapon.

*Crack!* It clashed against his parry. The force jarred up my arm.

I swung at his opposite leg, flinging the stave wildly once that was blocked too. His shoulder, his midriff, his head. My muscles already started to burn.

Calyse's mouth formed an O when I got the stick close to his cheek. Our two staves crossed there by his ear. "Tut tut," he said. "It's bad form to kill someone who's looking out for you."

I swung again and he parried every time. The *crack crack crack* echoed in my ears and rattled my teeth. Frustration built inside me. Shouldn't I be able to get one hit? With a yell, I barreled toward him, swinging.

But he wasn't there. I struck empty air. A surprised scream burst out of me when I was grabbed from behind, a wooden pole laid flush across my neck.

After a moment, the pressure on my neck released and Calyse stepped out from behind me, far too smug. "You see, that's—"

I smacked him hard in the hip with my stave.

He barely winced. "I deserved that."

But my pent-up anger wasn't finished. I widened the distance between my fists and shoved him in the chest. I still wanted to hit him while he was resisting. I was a flurry of movement, but I was getting nowhere. I couldn't strike him.

"Breathe," he said.

I kept on.

"Stop. Breathe." This time it was a command. I'd never heard that tone from him. For the first time, I heard the military commander in him.

When I wound up once more, he twisted the stave away from me and caught my wrists. The weapon thunked uselessly across the floor. He threw his own beside it and drew me close to him so my bound fists lay against his chest. I struggled as he held me pinned against him, but he was too solid. His strong arms had me too firmly in place.

"Breathe, crazy human girl." This time, the laugh was back in his tone.

Finally, my hot blood began to cool. The rage subsided. I wilted against his shoulder, snuffing up that smell of amber now mixed with musky sweat, though he didn't seem half as spent as I was. Maybe if I demonstrated I was no threat now, he would release me. But he kept me there a while longer, until I felt the heavy beating of his heart and the rise of his stomach as he breathed.

This was comfortable, and I was in need of closeness. In fact, I wanted to be closer.

My pulse jumped as I realized the unwanted feelings coursing through my body. I wriggled again to get out of his grasp and this time he responded. I stepped back.

"What was that?" I demanded.

"A brief but strenuous sparring session, I'd say."

"And then?"

"And then you weren't listening. Do you remember what I said would happen if you didn't listen?" He stepped forward cautiously, as though I were a feral cat.

He reached for my hand. I whipped it away.

"Let me show you something," he explained, forehead scrunched upward in a decidedly non-threatening and non-seductive way.

Reluctantly, I showed him my hand. When he held it up, blood was running down the side of my thumb.

"Shall I lick it off for you?"

At my disgusted exclamation, he threw back his head and laughed.

❧   6   ❧

Laura invited me to her massive royal suite the next day. There was an entire sitting area among the low-lit archways and columns. Upon a platform sat the largest bed I'd ever seen, surrounded by gauzy fabric. The same curtains drew across what sounded like a bubbling spring. Our house in Selene could easily have fit inside the room.

"This is wonderful, Laura," I breathed.

Her smile was more self-assured than I remembered. We sat across from each other at a little round table. "Thank you. Isn't it? I've missed our little room sometimes, though."

I swallowed thickly. I used to hold Laura in our bed, her protective older sister making sure nothing happened to her. Because of my rash actions that day, we could never return to that room. "I do too." I tried to banish my rising regret. "You must have some fun here," I said, waggling my eyebrows. "Endymion is utterly gorgeous, and he seems to love you very much."

"Lizzie!" But I got another smile, this time blushing and secret. "He does. We look out for each other." After a pause, she added cheekily, "And we do have a lot of fun here." Her eyes glazed before fixing once more on me. She reached out and drew my braid over my shoulder. "I could never get my braids to look like this."

I'd simply put it in a fishtail. "Yes, you can. I've seen you do it."

"The ends stick out."

I stroked my braid, simply looking at her. I loved her so much it hurt. That she didn't need me anymore was a new kind of hurt. I'd never stop wanting to look after her. "Yours look beautiful. And these—" Now I reached out, tapping the delicate ornament that encompassed the shell of her ear. I'd noticed something similar adorning Endymion earlier. "Are these only for the royal family or can I have one of these?"

She touched one absently. "They're like crowns, unfortunately. I don't think I can give you one. I wish I could." She grimaced apologetically. "How are you and Cal getting along?"

"I'm sure he'd love it if I called him that."

"He wouldn't mind."

"What about Callie?"

"He might mind that."

I grew serious. This was why she had asked to meet, not just to be sisters but with some agenda of fixing me. My hurt grew wider, though I couldn't have articulated why.

"I wish you'd let me figure things out in my own way instead of watching me all the time," I confessed. "There's... there's none left in the castle anymore, so there's no harm in letting me be free." I couldn't say the words out loud. I hated that there was no more fairy fruit here. Viscerally, it felt like a betrayal, and sometimes I couldn't convince my brain it wasn't.

Her lips pursed. "I worry about you, not just about that."

I dimly recalled crying on her shoulder. I set my jaw hard. "I'm fine."

"I want my Lizzie back." She gave a watery smile.

"I am your Lizzie."

She didn't respond.

ɩ❦ɪ

I ROLLED OVER AGAIN. THE SILK SHEETS FELT TOO COLD, THEN too hot. I couldn't get comfortable. Rest couldn't find me through the labyrinth of vague but acute concerns trapping me on every side.

In a huff, I sat up, defiant against the night. I hadn't seen Calyse when Laura had walked me back to the East Wing herself. Maybe he was still off composing pieces for flute. Good for him if he was. That meant I could take an uninterrupted walk to tire myself out enough to sleep.

Opening the door, I peeked out. Few lights were lit, but I didn't see his telltale shape in the darkness. I knew where the attendants left some extra blankets, so I snatched one and threw it around my shoulders. Most places here were cavernous, made of marble, stone, or wood. Unless a fire roared in the room, it felt cold to me.

I padded out, soles of my feet freezing, through the dining room and into a main artery of the castle, not sure where I was going. If I stayed in a relatively straight line, I could find my way back again.

The main area was much lighter, despite the late hour. Fae and forest creatures and goblin-looking men all traversed the walkways as though it were noon in the village. I kept my head down. I didn't want any attention, good or bad. I just wanted to walk and clear my mind.

A few minutes later, I decided to turn around and march the other way. Glowing eyes seemed to follow me everywhere, beautiful eyes, but unearthly. One pair might have been dark, but it could have been the shadows.

Right after I'd turned my back, I felt a finger tap my shoulder. "Lizzie? Is that you? Are you joking?"

I closed my eyes and slowly faced him.

A blurry and incredulous Calyse looked back at me, smelling of strong liquor. He scoffed. "I was gone a few hours in the middle of the night. You're worse than—" He cut himself off. "Let's get you to bed."

I shook him off. "I was just taking a walk."

"Then I'll walk with you." There was an unmistakable edge of irritation in his tone. "I thought it was safe to not think about you for a minute."

"It was. It is. You can go back to your drink if you want."

"S'done with that," he slurred.

"I don't need you to walk with me."

"A direc' order."

"Fine," I snapped, suddenly feeling more exhausted. I picked up the pace toward my bedroom, defeated.

We practically jogged back to the East Wing. No other women of Selene were loitering this late at night. Most of them still floated between reality and delusion as I had for several weeks. Compared to them, I functioned beautifully. I brought the blanket with me into my little cell.

Calyse charged into the room beside me. "I thought you were safe. I thought I could leave you alone," he said.

"You can."

"I can't!"

I felt like we'd had this argument a dozen times.

"Something would happen to you," he said.

"What would happen?" I sat on the bed and crossed my legs.

To my surprise, Calyse sat beside me. "I don't know," he

confessed sloppily. "But... I've seen the ones I'm supposed to protect... hurting, over and over." He dropped his eyes.

I bit my lip. "I've made mistakes like that too. Luckily," I laughed drily, "no one else needs us right now. They're all right." I knew that Calyse worked directly for King Endymion, so I supposed he might be talking about him. Together, Endymion and Laura seemed safe and happy.

He nodded stoutly. "They're all right," he repeated.

Neither of us seemed glad about that.

"I wish I could still protect her," I blurted.

Calyse's eyes shot to mine.

"I'm upset that I can't. I'm so upset. Does that make me selfish?" Why I was confiding in Calyse, I hadn't the faintest idea. Perhaps it was his drink-bleariness that made me think he wouldn't remember my confessions.

"Not selfish. Having a brother—or sister—is something special. You want to keep them for yourself. I do."

He missed Endymion too. The dark planes of his face looked soft in the dim light. Lines, barely visible, tightened at the edges of his full lips. Perhaps he understood a little.

Silence blanketed us, growing thick and giving me the time to notice the hard line of his jaw, the swell of muscle in his shoulder, nearly touching mine...

"I'm going to sleep," I announced, disconcerted.

"Finally." He came out of his stupor, knocking that muscular shoulder against mine. Already, the effect of the liquor was lessening. He stood. "You are the most trouble-prone girl I've ever met. Enough midnight walks, unless, for some reason, I'm there as well."

Thinking of the reason he might be with me at midnight made me tuck the covers to my chin as I said a hasty goodbye.

# ❧ 7 ❧

The woman beside me, ten years my senior, slurped her soup with concentration. My bad feelings from last night hadn't fully abated, leaving a thick veneer of loneliness, so I smiled at her.

"I'm sorry I haven't introduced myself," I said. We were all lonely, all struggling. Why should I see myself as better than any of them? If anything, they deserved more love and pity than I did, having been addicted and asleep longer.

My benchmate had brown hair, long and scraggly, and one of her pale eyelids looked swollen.

"I'm Lizzie. I'm from Selene, like you are, right?"

She turned her slow, dazed attention to me. "Selene, yes."

My attempt at a smile turned real. "Do you know the cottage closest to the woods? That's where I live. Lived."

"With the old women?"

My family was the only one in Selene made up entirely of women—four generations packed together inside that little cottage. In a village known for its maidens going missing, envy followed us and suitors followed me. I could tell her association with the house wasn't positive.

"Yes," I confirmed.

She took another deliberate sip of soup.

"And you are?"

"I?" She wavered, almost as if she couldn't remember. "I am Georgina."

Her name sounded somewhat familiar. She must have disappeared when I was only a child, but the names of those who had heeded the call of the forest echoed in the village for years afterward.

"Perhaps we could go for a walk some evening," I said, cheered by my own private defiance. Calyse didn't like that I walked at night to clear my mind. Well, then I could do it with someone else with whom I had more in common.

Georgina chewed her lip meditatively for a while. Her eyes had gone absent again. They glowed low like embers. "Do you know where we... could go?"

I understood her question perfectly. Fairy fruit. It was never far from any of our minds. I decided I wouldn't tell her it was all gone from the castle. "I thought just a walk to get some exercise, maybe talk for a bit."

Her swollen eye twitched with disappointment, but she sucked in a breath and answered, "Let's."

I patted her arm encouragingly, then turned back to my own soup. I could still help someone.

"Oh good. I stepped away and thought you might have fled for an exit," said Calyse, settling down next to me and pulling a large, vegetable-studded ham toward himself.

It wasn't rare for him to stop in to see how I was doing, but the other women had begun to notice his incessant hovering. It was embarrassing.

"Not before soup," I said archly. I flourished my spoon. *See, I'm eating.*

He smiled, though I'm sure he could tell his presence didn't delight me. Besides his rankling surveillance, I also hated the zing that crackled through my skin in the innocent places we touched. The bench was small for his big body, so his thigh rested against mine. So did his massive arm. I felt dwarfed and conspicuous. Other beings could elicit this response from me—not my jailer.

He took massive bites of the meat. I curled my lip in disgust.

Finally, he caught my look. "Still judging me for my diet, are you? How do you think I became like this?" He flexed his arm to demonstrate. The muscles were undeniably... impressive.

I blinked. "Being born Fae I thought was enough," I replied.

"It helps." He shoved more ham into his mouth. "I really am curious how you humans operate on so little. Or is it only you maidens?"

I disliked the term. "We were asleep for months or even years, so I don't think we are the best examples of humans as a whole."

He tipped his mouth. "Sounds fair."

When he finished his meal and we moved away from the table so as not to be overheard, I said in an undertone, "I think I would like to hit you again today."

"You're not sore from last time?" His eyes sparkled with a little too much mirth.

I was sore. My shoulders and biceps and sides ached, but that did nothing to lessen my resolve. "No."

His expression mocked my lie. "If that's what you want, we can go back."

"And I'm planning to take a walk this evening with a friend."

His brows rose. "A friend? You found someone you can stand to be with?"

Unexpectedly, the comment stung. "Yes. Georgina. She was

sitting on the other side of me. She needs a friend and I would like to know her better. Will that suit?"

He shrugged. "I have no order but to stare at your face whenever you choose to emerge, so that doesn't bother me," he said lightly.

The reminder did nothing to alleviate my mood. "Can I hit you now?"

He chuckled. "You can try."

❧

I DID TRY.

I let my swirling pain rise like oil to the surface as I lashed out, but just like last time, Calyse's defensive moves foiled every attempt I made to get near him.

The main part of the training area actually had running drills in it, so we moved to a smaller adjacent room intended for this kind of sparring. The floors felt spongier and the walls were draped with golden Fae heraldry.

"I like your spirit," he said, barely winded.

I, on the other hand, streamed with sweat and couldn't have spoken if I wanted to. If my sore muscles had ripped, I hardly would have been in more pain.

Finally, I halted my attack, trying to catch my breath. In an odd way, the pain felt good. Yes, my face no doubt looked as red as a poisonous mushroom and furious tears masqueraded as sweat down my face, but it felt good nonetheless. It was pain I could understand.

"Is that enough?" he asked, planting the stave next to him like a traveler's staff.

I shook my head and lifted the rod once more. Hot pain

seared through my side. I twisted sideways to combat the sting but it only lanced deeper. Dropping the stave, I winced.

Calyse was with me in an instant. "Not to worry," he said, his low voice practiced and soothing. I wondered how many times he had done this. "Just lie down. Bring your knees together, like that."

I grimaced as I lowered myself to the ground and rolled to my back. He crouched beside me and gently held the side of my knees, laying them down to one side. The knifing pain shot through me again.

"It's all right. It's all right. Just a sprain, it looks like. Not even a very bad one." He held my knees down and placed his other hand on my shoulder to keep me from rotating with my legs.

Once I was able to take a few deep breaths, he smirked at me. "I knew you were lying earlier. This is a lot of exertion if you're not used to it."

"I'm strong enough. I just..." But I didn't know what to say.

"Now I want you to roll onto your stomach."

Straightening my knees painfully, I did as he said.

Strong fingers explored my shoulders, massaging the muscle, and rotating my arms. His expert hands gave just the right pressure, knew where to go to address that sweet ache from the fight. My pulse beat harder everywhere. I didn't want him to stop. He dug into the muscle just behind my shoulder and I had to hold in an unseemly noise. He concentrated there for a while before moving my arm in precise ways, finally bringing both arms, fully extended, above my head. It was a worshipful position, full of abandon.

While I stretched out, his hands moved down to explore my side. I flinched when he began kneading my waist.

"Does that hurt?" he murmured.

"Not enough."

"You say such naughty things."

If he was trying to scandalize me again, it wasn't working. Seducing would be a better word. Surely, by now he could feel the pound of my heartbeat, the shallowness of my breath.

After all, was it so bad to want Calyse? In other moments, I could still despise him for keeping me under guard. For now, I longed for him to touch me everywhere.

I held still under his hands. At least I had this…

No. I wanted more. I'd let him know I wanted more.

Releasing a satisfied moan, I reached back for his arm. Immediately, he stopped massaging me.

Heart thundering, I sat up. The ache in my side had dwindled to a pleasant soreness.

Did his flirtations mean nothing after all? Had I just made a fool of myself?

On his knees, he eyed me warily, the ghost of a hesitant smile on his lips. "Well, you are an enigma. If you're trying to make me spend less time with you, that sound wasn't the way." His voice and chuckle were both husky.

Slowly, in case I was wrong, I crawled closer. He watched me hungrily as I propped myself up in front of him.

He narrowed his eyes roguishly. "I'm sorry, do you hate me or want me?"

"Both, sometimes," I admitted. "Is this all right?"

"If the lady wants."

When I leaned in against his broad chest, muscles clearly delineated even through the leather armor, he held me gently but firmly in place. His hand took up a good portion of my back.

His amber and smoke scent filled my lungs as I brought my face to his. His kiss made my body alight as if I felt him everywhere. His lips moved as his fingers had, searching, knowing just the right moment to dig in for more.

I moaned and settled even closer, straddling his lap. I felt him smile against my mouth. His lips opened under mine, inviting and erotic. I licked inside, and I felt the hard bulge of his trousers between my legs. Bold, I rocked against him, hanging onto his strong back as I ground hard against his erection. The motion teased my ache, raised my pulse.

Calyse's arms felt like rock, unmoving, as though he feared that if he submitted to this growing pleasure he would crush me. Finally, he raised one upward and wrapped my braid around one fist, tugging my head back.

I released a cry. I didn't slow the rolling of my hips as he bent to kiss my neck. Kissing became biting when I bucked right over the spot where I was wettest. He groaned, holding the very place by my neck where his fingers had massaged but this time with his teeth.

"Yes," I said, letting him know I enjoyed this. He wasn't hurting me. To punctuate my word, I thrust hard against him.

I earned a loud groan and an extra tug on my braid. His tongue traced a path along the bitemarks and up to the soft spot beneath my chin. Now he was thrusting back up into me, little movements, almost involuntary. I gasped as he hit my pulsing ache just right.

With a feral growl, he swept me to the floor, his huge body on top of me. He kept his weight off me except for where he crushed me with his lips and thrust against me hard and insistent between my legs. I kept them spread, inviting more pressure to fill my pulsing need. My wet undergarments were surely soiling his armor from such firm, demanding rubbing.

After a few more minutes, Calyse let out a mighty groan and I knew it was over. He brought his lips to mine one more time, then rolled to lay beside me.

Still breathing heavily, he grinned at me, shaking his head. "I didn't expect *that* to happen today," he said.

"And we still have our clothes on." I felt bleary and achy and very good.

He laughed. "Imagine if we hadn't."

I already was. "Calyse." I didn't know when this idea had started, but now that it was here, it didn't feel new. "I enjoyed that."

"Naturally."

"Don't ruin it. I was thinking, what if we..." An odd shyness crept up on me. Laura was the shy one, not me. "What if we... helped each other? I need a distraction and you"—I eyed his full lips, the muscles in his torso—"you are a very good distraction. As aggravating as you can be, we both... need someone. Not forever. But for now."

"Are you asking me for regular sex?"

I scrunched my face. "Yes."

"Well..." He placed one hand behind his head and looked wistfully at the ceiling. "I'm not opposed to a little excitement." He sighed. "You have more fire in you than I thought, human girl."

"Just call me Lizzie."

"Not my sweet nemesis?"

"Lizzie's fine."

"I like nemesis too."

❧    8    ❧

I wore a scarf on my walk that evening. Calyse, blessedly, gave Georgina and me some space, walking a little behind.

No matter how good it had been with him in the little sparring room—good enough to leave tender marks on my neck I felt sure appeared as bright red welts—ours wasn't a relationship. It was a deal, something to comfort us. Secretly, our encounters were also a way to speed my apparent recovery until I could finally get back to fairy fruit, freedom, or both. If I seemed healthy and happy, Laura and the King would release me from Calyse's everlasting watchfulness. It was a paradoxical arrangement, but, for now, it worked for me.

I convinced Georgina to wear one of the gowns Laura had given all the women in the East Wing. She looked lovely in a coral dress with long sleeves and a slight train. Her hair still hung limp past her shoulders and her dry skin flaked, but a bit of pink bloomed in her pale cheeks that hadn't been there before.

"How much of the castle have you seen?" I asked, keeping my tone light. Existence as one of the "sleeping maidens" was a dreary one.

"Not very much."

"There are some beautiful areas."

That was one topic gone.

"Do you have any family I might know back in Selene?" It was a sensitive subject, but at least I might be able to get more than a couple words from her.

As usual, beautiful Fae and downy or feathered forest creatures capered by us, always engaged in some business or pleasure. Above us soared ceilings I previously couldn't have imagined.

Georgina observed none of it. In fact, her pensive expression deepened to a frown.

"I'm sorry," I said. "I didn't mean—"

"I wasn't tricked."

I wasn't prepared for that outburst. "Pardon?"

"I wasn't tricked. I chose to go into the forest. I did this to myself." Her voice—a little raspy from lack of speaking—sounded like a confession.

I touched her shoulder gently. "That's all right. You didn't know."

"I did. I wanted them to take me." She still wasn't looking at me, but at something deep within that had been festering in her soul.

I let my fingers slip down to my side again, waiting for the rest.

"I knew there could be forest creatures or Fae or any manner of thing, and I would have taken any of it. It wasn't fair. Not to me, not to my son. But I did it anyway. And I would do it again." The monotony of words rose defiantly.

Something in her confession echoed in my own soul. I, too, had plunged into the woods without hearing the famous call to buy the fruit. I had become engaged to James the baker so my family would have enough food to eat and Laura had scorned my sacrifice. I was hurt and angry. I too could blame no one else.

"Why did you want to be taken?" I asked, as mildly as I could.

She licked her dry lips. I knew what she was thinking. In retrospect, it seemed to be about the fairy fruit, its achingly blissful taste, but we hadn't known that until later.

"It was my husband," she finally answered. "I thought anything in the world would be better than him. Even my son couldn't make me stay." That was the first time that true regret passed over her features.

What a shame that Georgina had no one but a stranger to confide in now. Despite my awkwardness, I said, "Your son. Who's he?"

"Gabriel."

"Gabriel, the sheriff?"

She looked me in the eye for the first time. "He was six when I left him," she said oddly. "Is he grown now? Has it been that long?" Her dry face looked ashen, but her golden eyes burned with intensity.

"He's the only Gabriel I know," I said. "He has six children. He lives in the best cottage in the village."

A sob gasped from her mouth.

If Georgina was Gabriel's mother, then she was much older than I'd first thought. The enchanted sleep had preserved a version of her youth.

The oldest "maidens" appeared to be little more than decaying corpses. How old must they be? The revelation shook me.

"He seems like he's doing well," I continued. "His daughter Harriet is a friend of mine."

"Now what would he think?" she muttered. "He would not know his mother's eyes."

My heart squeezed. "They're beautiful eyes." I stroked the

side of her head with my fingertips, catching a few strands of hair and placing them behind her ear.

She stopped to face me. "I haven't looked. Are mine gold or black?" She battled discomfort to flutter her gaze up to mine as a disobedient child might.

"Gold. What do you mean 'gold or black'? When have you seen black eyes?" Blood grew louder in my ears. The only black eyes I'd seen were on the bird woman who had led me to fairy fruit.

Georgina waved a listless hand. "Some of the women..."

I waited, but she provided no end to that statement. Her confession had obviously tired her. Setting my jaw in frustration, I saw I would get no further answers tonight. Together we turned around to head back to the East Wing.

Calyse, that mountain, stood conspicuously in front of us now. He waited for us to pass before following again. As we walked abreast of him, he caught my eye and made a face. Strangely, I knew immediately what he meant.

*Not the most thrilling company.*

I shot back an answering expression. *You're wrong. She's struggling but our walk wasn't that bad.*

He smiled.

৩৯৩

With Georgina safely in bed, I had a decision to make. Heart-pounding awkwardness quickly settled between me and Calyse in the dark as I padded my way back to my room. Too many emotions—excitement, discomfort, regret—churned for me to make sense of them. I sensed him following me, though his footsteps didn't make a sound.

When I reached my door, I turned around, throat dry. "I don't know... You don't have to..." My fumbling only made my cheeks heat.

In the dim light, Calyse looked like a big shadow. A big, smiling shadow who didn't seem half as nervous as I was.

Never before had I requested something so outrageous as I had with him, but he'd made it easy. He didn't judge me or laugh it off or act disgusted. But now, out of the heat of the moment, I doubted if sex with Calyse was the best idea.

"You're right," he said, "we don't have to. If you changed your mind—"

"I don't... I..." Could I be any more flustered? My neck under the scarf grew hotter.

He let out a breathy laugh. "Whatever you want is fine."

The pause that followed while I stared at him in the dark seemed unending. He acted completely impervious to my awkwardness, not so much as shifting his weight. His eyes, which glowed slightly, showed how much my hesitation amused him.

I shoved him. "Stop laughing!"

"I'm not laughing. You see why I call you little nemesis—always resorting to violence." He hadn't so much as wobbled when I pushed him.

Suddenly resolved, I puffed out my chest. "I'm not tired. Let's go somewhere else."

The idea of the other women hearing our... activities didn't appeal to me. Plus, I felt antsy.

"Anywhere in particular?" he asked, walking beside me as I stalked madly out of the East Wing. One of his steps matched two of mine, although I wasn't short for a girl.

"You're the one who knows this castle."

"And you're the one charging toward... nowhere, I guess. Follow me."

We threaded through scarred and furred faces. None of them

knew our secret. And none of their eyes were black. Georgina's revelation niggled in the back of my mind, insistent as fairy fruit, but those misgivings were quickly being overtaken by anticipation. Where were we going?

Revelers and passersby parted to make way for Calyse's huge form. He moved easily, but I had gotten a taste of how skilled that body was at combat. He was not a being to take lightly, even if he sometimes took himself that way. My body warmed at the thought.

He led me to an area of the castle I'd never t seen before, which wasn't saying much since I'd seen so little. We ascended a tightly winding staircase. Twice we plastered ourselves against the wall to make way for others coming down. This was especially hard for Calyse. The steps rose so many stories I began to get dizzy and my legs burned. The sprain in my side started throbbing.

My breath gusted out in short bursts by the time we crested the top. A slim window reached from floor to ceiling in the little circular room. From it, dark trees stretched below us like a sea. Large pillows scattered across the floor. One lantern, suspended in metalwork depicting a crescent moon, hung in the center of the space.

A lookout, or a lover's nest. Both, probably.

"Do people come up here very often?" I asked, peering out the window. Stars splashed the night sky above.

"Sometimes they do." His devilish grin set my heart beating harder. "You said you wanted excitement."

I could hardly breathe. I did want excitement, but this felt utterly wanton, wickedly Fae.

"You can still say no."

"I don't want to say no."

His mouth curled upward as he approached me by the

window. "You don't want to say no?" He touched my temple with a fingertip, drawing idle circles there. He lowered his voice. "You're very... *little*. Just let me know if I'm hurting you."

By now I felt my pulse in my stomach. I nodded, unwrapping my scarf.

His eyes lit up. Evidently, I was right. There were marks, and he had made them.

"Hopefully," he said, languorously wrapping his arms around me and burrowing his face in my neck, "no one will come up and see."

After kissing each of the dark spots on my neck, Calyse straightened and unbuckled his knife belt. He set the weapon gently against the wall. My skin fizzed with the memory of his lips. I searched hungrily for the openings or clasps on his clothes, but the tight-fitting leather armor seemed bound to his body. Only the belt looked easy to remove. My hands roved to find the weakness myself.

He gazed down at me teasingly as I ran my fingers over his chest and sides and powerful back, his hips, his ass, his thighs. For a moment I forgot what I was searching for. His form under my hands mesmerized me.

"This is why we have attendants," he murmured, reaching behind to some hidden fastening at his neck. "It's far too difficult to remove."

He stopped after loosening the neck guard. It flopped forward, revealing the hollow of his throat. I wanted to press my tongue into it, to suck him like fairy fruit.

"But you," he said, closing his hands around my waist and

squeezing upward until he reached my breasts, dress rising with his motion, "not as difficult."

He thumbed my breasts, teasing the nipples under the fabric. The bottom of my gown rose to the level of my undergarments. I gripped the edge of the skirt and Calyse helped me haul it over my head.

He was right. I was little compared to him. I'd always been thin, but now I bordered on malnourished. Until now, I hadn't cared that my breasts had grown smaller.

But the giant Fae warrior gazed appreciatively at me, so appreciatively than I edged off my underwear as well.

He looked... delighted.

"Help me with this," he said with an edge of urgency to his voice. He turned his back to me and crouched a bit so I could find the rest of the hidden clasps. Once I had undone them to the middle of his back, he reached behind and undid the rest at once. The entire top piece stripped off his body, revealing bulging patterns of muscle under smooth dark skin. He got the trousers off himself.

His intoxicating scent filled the room, inviting me to lose myself. Without hesitation, he took my face and kissed me, our bodies colliding. My guts somersaulted at the press of his chest, his abdomen, his muscular thighs against mine. It felt like being taken by a wave, the overwhelming strength pulling me under.

I was speechless, hungry. We tripped on a pillow and fell, I on top of him. I sat up, straddling his waist. His beauty stunned me, bringing blood to my cheeks. He dragged me down with a roguish look.

"Already wet," he whispered, rolling so he was on top of me. The strong fingers that had massaged my shoulders and side pressed the inside of my thighs to spread me wider. That wasn't where I wanted those fingers. He caressed my leg teasingly, avoiding where I pulsed for contact. Slickness had dripped down my leg, and he avoided those spots too. Instead, he rotated my hips just a little wider, testing them almost as he had done my arm.

"Calyse," I demanded, but it came out a whimper. I flung my arms around his back to pull him down on me, but he stayed firm.

"Patience," he said, bringing his finger maddeningly close to my entrance before moving away. He watched my face, clearly enjoying the torture he was putting me through.

I stuck my tongue out at him and bucked my hips at just the right moment that he brushed me. Still no pressure where I ached to have it.

He continued to stroke my legs until I thought I would go mad. Sweat sheened my chest at the strain of waiting for pleasure.

"Calyse," I ground out again.

"Is there something you want?"

I could have screamed at his nonchalant attitude. I knew he wanted me too. His large, stiff cock resting against my leg told the truth. "Touch me."

"Like this?" He stopped caressing my thigh to squeeze my breast, sucking the nipple into his mouth. He flicked his tongue over it.

I gasped and writhed. "More."

He gave it a little bite then did the same with the other.

I reached down to guide him into me but he moved away. I growled with frustration.

"More?" he asked. "You mean like this?" Finally his long fingers met my wet center, stroking down the center.

I moaned.

"Or like this?"

He teased the sensitive nub with his thumb while guiding two fingers inside me. They pulsed in tandem.

"Oh god!" I arched back against the pillow, gripping the edge of it.

He increased the pressure, the speed, added another finger inside me. I expanded to that one delicious, aching point on my body. I drenched him, losing all sense of myself. Rocking up against him to rub harder against that spot, I fell apart with a cry, contracting in and trembling outward again.

He kissed me, smiling, and painted my belly with his soaked fingers. "Hands and knees," he commanded. "I don't want to crush you."

Delirious, I did as he said. I looked behind me to see him on his knees, all his strength on full display. He pushed against my entrance.

If he was going to tease me again, I wouldn't have it. I backed into him, felt him sliding into me, further, further.

He groaned as I leaned fully against him. He gripped my hips for leverage and thrust hard, smacking my behind with the force. Finding a violent rhythm, he grunted and pressed and slapped. The furtive sounds were hypnotic.

He snatched my braid as he had done in the training room. I released a groan of pleasure as he hauled me up firmly.

He held me against his chest, one hot hand fondling my breast, as he continued to thrust up into me. "You like it a little rough, don't you?" he panted in my ear.

I'd never admitted it to anyone before, but I did. "Yes."

He set me back down on my hands, gave me a slap, and went harder, deeper. A large hand slid down my back, pressing my cheek into the pillow, even as he drove into me. I whimpered, needing more of this sensation, more of him taking control, losing himself even as he was taking what he wanted.

"Still all right?" he grunted.

I let out a cry of ecstasy.

The heel of his hand on my upper back grew heavier. He gripped my shoulder to pull himself deeper into me.

"Ah, yes!"

His arm began to shake more with each of my cries, his thrusts more frenzied.

With a yell, he leaned back, letting go of me. His orgasm wet the pillows.

Sweat plastered my hair against my forehead as I lay there, pleasantly exhausted and panting. Calyse, still on his knees, chest heaving, took a moment to regain his senses.

"We're not bad at that," he said through strained breaths.

I slowly pushed myself up. "You're a little disgusting, though," I teased, eyeing the soiled pillows.

"And you're a dirty little nemesis."

I caught my breath for a few more beats.

"Will that serve as enough of a distraction for you?" he asked, with a look of complete confidence.

I threw one of the smaller pillows at him in answer.

❧ 10 ❧

"Get behind me," Calyse whispered, flipping over the soiled pillow and standing near the window.

Perhaps it wouldn't do to have the Queen's sister found in such a compromising position. I doubted anyone in this castle—apart from the women of Selene—would think much of it.

Still, I tucked myself behind him, between his body and the wall. I couldn't help but laugh at the ridiculousness of our situation. There was no way for him to don his complicated leather armor before the visitor arrived in the turret room. My clothes, I realized, also lay among the pillows, but they were so much smaller that perhaps they wouldn't be noticed.

Calyse completely blocked me, so I couldn't see who crested the rise. A sultry feminine voice sighed in disappointment rather than surprise at seeing him there, then the steps retreated.

I burst out of my hiding place. "That was not subtle."

"Subtlety is not a strength of mine," he admitted.

"Who was that?" I'd heard that voice before. It hurtled my thoughts back along forbidden tracks.

"I don't know," he said, putting on his trousers.

"It wasn't the woman with red hair and black eyes?"

He stilled, even his breath halted. Slowly, he turned his face to me with an expression sharper than any I'd seen from him. "Black eyes," he repeated.

I found my clothes and put them back over my head. "Yes, the woman with the bird—"

"What do you mean, 'black eyes'?"

Was he accusing me of something? His demeanor had shifted into that of a soldier sensing an imminent threat. Did he know she led me to the fairy fruit?

"Her eyes were black," I answered, at a loss. "There was no color inside."

He opted to take his knife belt rather than his molded shirt before jumping toward the stairs. "Come. You'll tell me everything."

"I—" But he was already descending. I followed after, wrapping my scarf in place.

"When did you see this woman?" came his voice from somewhere below.

"The other day."

"Fae?"

"Yes."

"Where?"

"At the party."

Calyse was almost too far away to hear now, even though I tripped down as quickly as I could after him. We passed the Fae woman and her companion, who almost toppled in out speed.

"Have you seen anyone else who looked like that?"

Out of breath, I slowed. "No." Then I remembered something. "Georgina has, though, or else she's seen the same person I did."

"Hurry, Lizzie!"

I was rushing as fast as I could. Why couldn't he wait a moment? What was so urgent? I pursed my lips and tried to increase my pace. He obviously would have left me behind if he could, our intimate encounter all but forgotten.

Dizziness gripped me when I reached the bottom. All that whirling around and around the corkscrew steps made me waver. Calyse eyed me darkly, all his body tense.

"Come on," he said and charged away.

I ran after him but my limbs were sore from the week's exertion. A jog I would never have considered difficult in Selene now wore me down. I wasn't strong enough yet to follow at his pace.

"What is the matter?" I demanded.

"We need to see the King immediately."

It wasn't an answer, but my blood grew cold. Sucking in air, I glanced side to side, searching for the bird woman, but she wasn't there.

"Do you know her name?"

I couldn't answer. I could hardly move my feet in front of each other.

Once again, Calyse halted to wait for me, his resentment for the delay obviously growing. "All right?" he asked, but his face was hard.

My chest heaved. I refused to say I couldn't keep up, but we both knew it. He was a warrior, used to training. I'd been asleep for weeks and malnourished after that. I was improving, but slowly.

"Do you know her name?" he asked again.

I shook my head. She hadn't told me.

"Did she talk to you?"

I hesitated. He didn't know she was the one who had led me to the kitchens? His manner was so urgent I felt compelled to tell him the truth in case the bird woman was a murderer or something.

Calyse walked purposefully—slower this time—toward the royal wing. I finally realized where we were going.

To speak to the King himself.

"Yes," I managed.

"Tell the King everything she said to you. Don't tell me now."

This authoritative version of Calyse grated on me. If I didn't think I was baggage before this, I knew it now.

By the time we reached the King's bedchamber, I had to hold the wall to keep from stumbling.

Calyse didn't so much as knock before entering through the molded double doors. "End!" he cried.

I followed, closing the doors behind us.

"End! Where are you?"

I couldn't fathom what could be important enough to sprint shirtless to the King's bedchamber to tell him.

A small splash drew my attention to the gauzy veil on the left-hand side of the huge space. Calyse heard it too, because he tore over and ripped the fabric to the side.

In the alcove, Endymion reclined in a circular bath sunk into the floor, large enough for two people to float horizontally end to end. A male attendant rubbed oil into his shoulders. Apart from a slight narrowing of his eyes, Endymion didn't betray any surprise at seeing Calyse there, urgent and half-dressed.

"Cal. Is Lizzie all right?"

I felt half-dead, but Calyse ignored the question.

"The Enemy. The Enemy might be here."

Endymion leaned back further, at ease. "Impossible. Not after what happened that night." His carved lips even gave a bitter smile.

Calyse's hand wandered to his knife hilt. Did he even realize he was doing it? "I thought so too, but Lizzie and one of the other girls have seen *black eyes* here in the castle." He moved to give me the opportunity the speak.

I had no idea what to say. I still didn't understand what was going on.

The King regarded me with insolent beauty, the quintessential Fae lord.

"She... was the one who led me to the kitchens. Her eyes were black."

"The kitchen where you ate the fairy fruit."

My cheeks flamed, but I jutted my chin and stood tall. Next to Calyse's form, that didn't feel tall at all. "Yes."

"Cal." The King's voice was conciliatory. "Your job is done. You've done more than I should ever have asked of you. Rest now. Look after Laura's sister."

"End, I believe her."

He flicked his long fingers toward the ceiling. "Dim light." The attendant kept moving his hands hypnotically over Endymion's shoulders. "There is no threat within our walls. Don't seek out enemies where there are none."

Calyse's expression was brutal. "I know the Shadow—"

"But did you see this yourself?"

A pause. "No."

"You deserve a rest, a... simpler assignment." The King's languid eyes moved momentarily to me.

Cal's eyes dropped, profound frustration and disappointment there. My belly twisted.

Without a word, Calyse strode from the room. I found myself once again hurrying after him, but, after a few steps, I slowed. Why should I run after someone who clearly would rather be anywhere else but with me? According to him, there were far more important things to deal with than to watch a recovering human girl.

Bitterness coated my tongue. Not only did Calyse act resentful of his new post, but Endymion dismissed me as well. Just because I craved fairy fruit didn't mean I couldn't tell black from other colors. The implication was insulting. These Fae males and their arrogance...

I arrived at the East Wing minutes after Calyse and marched right past him to my room.

"I believe you," he said. I heard the same tone as the interrogation behind those words. He wasn't apologizing. He was continuing the far more important work of uncovering this potential threat, whatever it was. "The King just doesn't—"

I closed the door in his face.

My craving for fairy fruit prevented me from sleeping. Choosing Calyse as a distraction was a foolish idea. Now, I felt like more of a burden than ever. The Fae woman with black eyes consumed his thoughts, not his duty to me.

I didn't emerge until the midday meal, bleary and heartsick and angry. Calyse waited outside, as he always did, though he'd exchanged his leathers for a breezy brown shirt and green trousers, tight against his biceps. He left the thick strands of his hair down. As always, he wore the knife at his belt.

"Morning," he said.

"Nice to see you have a shirt on today," I bit out, not looking at him.

I found the communal dining area and sat next to Georgina. "You mentioned yesterday that you had seen someone with all-black eyes," I said without preamble. "Do you remember who they were?"

Her vacant gaze drifted from me to the space above my shoulder. "He already asked me about that this morning. Is it that important?"

Bristling, I reached for a honey-soaked bun. "I doubt it." The food tasted like paste as I chewed.

Calyse sat beside me.

"Is there anyone else you can watch besides me?" I asked, finally whirling on him. "See all these women? None of them have a fighter assigned to them. Why am I the only captive?"

"You're the Queen's sister." He didn't add more. Maybe he didn't know the reason himself.

Disgusted, I took one more bite and gave up my attempt to finish my meal.

"Lizzie," he said, following me.

Good, he could chase me instead of the other way around.

"Lizzie!" He laid a hand on my shoulder and turned me to face him. "Did I do something to anger you?" Traces of concern showed themselves in the tilt of his lip, the corner of his eye.

Curse me, but my body realized we were alone in the space next to my bedroom. Uninvited memories returned of his powerful hands and his husky voice whispering, "You like it a little rough, don't you?" My warming skin just made me more furious.

"You've made it abundantly clear that I'm just a burden to you. You wouldn't even explain why you were so worried last night. You just stormed off and expected me to run after you." I couldn't form my thoughts into more words, so I cut myself off, breath gusting hard from my lungs.

"It was an urgent matter—"

"Apparently it was. Will you tell me now what all that meant?"

His neck contracted as he swallowed. "I can't explain it fully."

"Because I might have only seen the woman in dim light?" I snarled.

He sighed and rolled his eyes. "The King doesn't want to

believe there could be a threat inside the castle. But I believe you.
I believe you."

"Then why can't you explain?"

His jeweled gaze held mine. "I've kept his secret for a hundred years. I can't break that now." His cheek moved in a half-smile of apology.

A shiver ran up my spine.

"You need more to eat," he proclaimed.

I opened my mouth to protest.

"I'll get you something good." With a wink, he trotted back to the dining area. He returned with a hand pie filled with meat and gravy.

His choice almost made me smile. It was so typical of him.

"Munch on this." Leaning in to speak in my ear, he added, "And talk to the other women. See if they've seen the same thing. More voices might get Endymion to listen."

He lingered there too long to be innocent. His breath warmed my neck. The anticipation of secrets charged the tiny space between his lips and my ear.

When he pulled back, he wore the ghost of a smile.

I released a breath and took a bite of the hand pie. It wasn't bad. "I'm sure I'm not the only one."

"Your sister was good at investigations. Perhaps it runs in your blood."

I longed to know what Calyse meant by that, but I was proud of Laura for earning the compliment. "I taught her everything."

"Oh," he laughed, "then let's show that stubborn bastard the truth. You, of course, may never call him that, but the two of us are brothers."

I matched his mock-piety with my own. "I understand."

As I finished my meal, which had regained a little flavor, I met two more women. After realizing that Georgina must have been in her sixties, I didn't trust my eyes. Even women who appeared my own age could be far older.

One couldn't look me in the eye and didn't seem to understand my question. I didn't even discover her name, but despite my frustration, a profound wave of pity filled me to look at her. She had blonde hair, as I did, freckles, as Laura did, and her eyes were infinitely sad.

The other said her name was Eve. Her lucidity surprised me, because she had white streaks in her hair and open sores on the backs of her hands. Who knew how long she had lain in that room with us? She said the maidens' eyes sometimes flashed black before returning to normal, but I found myself doubting her story as Endymion had doubted mine.

Already tired, I headed back to my room. Only then did I realize that Calyse hadn't followed me around for my unsuccessful interviews. He must have briefly abandoned his post to storm off in search of more enemies.

In my doorway, I halted. Calyse sat on my bed, hands in his lap. Never before had he come in while I wasn't there. At least, not that I knew.

"What...?"

He lifted his chin to urge me inside. I closed the door.

"I didn't find out anything to help," I said. My next words were strangled by my realization that Calyse's hands were tied at the wrists.

"That's all right. There are plenty to ask," he said, nonchalant, as though he wasn't tied up in my room.

"What...?" I began again.

He lifted his bound hands, expression turning wicked. "I'm sorry for yesterday. The eyes you've seen—they are a problem, but you are my primary responsibility right now. I should not have made you feel like a captive. Frankly, this assignment is a... shift for me, but you are not at fault for how I feel. We'll search out the truth together. Meantime, we are both here for good reason."

I gazed at him, relieved and puzzled. He still wasn't giving me answers, but he was offering a truce.

"That doesn't explain what you're doing here," I said slowly, indicating the bonds.

"You felt like a captive so I'm offering you some control. Captive for captive."

My pulse jumped. Only yesterday we had coupled for the first time and already I wanted more. Looking at his wrists, I knew he could break the ties he'd used to bind himself, but he was offering submission. Never had I wielded control like this, certainly not over men, especially Fae warriors built like a bull.

My breath was shallow as I said, "I don't want the other women to hear."

"I'll stay quiet if you will." His molten gaze invited me to do my worst.

I growled quietly with frustration as I gave into temptation. "Anything?" I whispered.

"I doubt you'll be too rough for me."

My stomach swooped as he grinned.

"I'm still angry, you know." I found the buckle of his trousers and opened it.

"If you weren't, you wouldn't be my nemesis."

He watched as I peeled down his pants and pulled out his cock.

"No sound," I reminded him, and squeezed hard, yanking upward with some of my frustration.

His cry turned into an uneven chuckle, aroused and almost nervous.

I pumped down, then up again with more force.

"That's it," he rasped, letting his head tip back.

I found a rhythm, pulling and twisting at the tip, that satisfied my fury and my desire. Only the faintest sounds of caught breath escaped from him as he grew harder under my hand. I felt him flex upward to meet me.

"That's enough," I muttered, intoxicated with power.

He exhaled, bringing his head up to reveal eyes so dilated I only saw the faintest rim of gold. His sultry mouth was open, ready for my next move.

I had merely been wearing my identical white dress, but I removed it in full sight of Calyse, watching his expression the entire time. I saw when fascination turned to hunger, his eyes roving over my stiff breasts and down. I would give him some of the agony he gave me yesterday.

"Lie down," I commanded. "Loop your hands around the bedpost."

The bed had four thin posts at its corners. Calyse lay diagonally, massive arms above his head, so he could fulfil my instructions. His helpless position only enflamed me more.

I tugged off his trousers the rest of the way.

"Head back," I said.

He pressed it into the mattress, exposing that spot of skin I'd wanted to lick, right at the hollow of his throat. I shoved his shirt up around his forearms before pressing my tongue at the base of his neck. He tasted salty with hints of sweet amber. I sucked up more of the flavor of his skin, scraping my teeth across his throat.

A reverberation from him shuddered against my mouth. I smiled. How wild could I make him feel? Could I make him beg for me as I had begged for him?

I straddled his waist and leaned down to speak into his ear, making sure my pert nipples brushed his firm, exposed skin. His breathing became a little less regular. I slid back just enough to touch his cock before he returning. "How much do you want me?" I whispered.

He gave me a look that chastised me for sweet cruelty.

"How much?"

"Must I tell you?"

"Yes."

He adjusted his arms. "Do you want detail?"

Desire throbbed between my legs. "Yes."

"Ever since the training ground, I want to fuck you up against a wall every time I see you. And now, I want to be so deep inside you that you forget where you are. I want to bother the others. So ride me."

My breathing came ragged, but I whispered, "I'm the one in charge." Either he was trying to appease me by fulfilling my fantasy or he felt the carnal pull between us too. I wanted to believe it was both. Calyse was my jailer, but he knew how to make my blood pump hot and my skin tingle.

"Ooh," he scolded.

I traced my hands idly down his firm chest in answer. "Maybe I won't at all."

His smirk twisted into a grimace.

I rubbed myself against him, rolling my hips, hitting one spot that I needed. I took my time, changing positions until I held onto his arms, my breasts near his face.

"Lizzie."

I let out a broken sigh as I ground against him.

"Lizzie."

His urgent whisper sounded pained. He was begging. I grew wetter, taking another few thrusts to torture him.

"Damn it. Lizzie!"

"Shhh." I kissed him as I'd wanted to for a while, arching against him. He responded with open-mouthed passion.

When I broke the kiss, I bit his ripe lip before sliding down his hips. His erection was rock hard, punctuated with veins. A guttural sound escaped him as I settled on top of him, burying him deep inside me. I was so slick that it took no adjusting to bring him fully inside. I bit back a groan and began rocking hard, finding the places that still ached to be touched. The movement pressed Calyse's body back and forth on the bed, mussing his thick strands of hair. He looked beautiful and wild and sweat-slicked. I didn't take either of us long to find release.

When it was over, I replaced my clothes a little awkwardly and unbound him from the bed. What I really wanted was to lie on his chest and for him to hold me as I fell asleep so I might dream of something other than fairy fruit and the confines of my cage, but that wasn't part of our arrangement. We lusted for each other, offered one another a diversion from our distasteful situations, but that was it. We could hardly even be called friends. Allies, perhaps, but only in the context of shared distraction and our search for the black-eyed woman.

"Thank you," I said, immediately cringing.

Dimples appeared in his smile. He tousled his hair into better order. "You're absolutely wicked." Then, quieter, "Sleep short. I'll see you tomorrow."

few days later, Laura came to visit.

Calyse evidently had a few hours off because a new guard—silent and tall, with hair brighter red than the bird woman had—stood watch outside my door. It chafed that he could leave while I never could. Every few days he had a short reprieve from his duties. I strongly suspected that he used his time to look into the perceived threat rather than to relax. His jovial face always appeared more shadowed than it had before he left.

"I've brought you something," Laura said, producing a flask with blue liquid inside.

I took it and swirled the contents around the little cylinder.

"It's a potion. I thought it might be able to help you rest, maybe to think of other things."

Other things besides fairy fruit.

I clasped the little bottle in my fist. "Thank you. You were always good at making these. Do you still garden?"

"Sometimes."

If she had done any gardening today, it didn't show. She wore a black dress seemingly made of strategically placed ribbons. Gold ornaments fixed them in place. It was both richer and more sensual than anything she would have worn back in Selene.

Personally, I wore one of the outfits she had sent me, this one a deep, rusty orange silk with a beveled skirt. It made me feel like an autumn leaf or a fire. It reminded me of Calyse's eyes.

I unstoppered the bottle. Our easy rapport had vanished like smoke since we had both been taken. She had married Endymion and I had fallen into enchanted sleep followed by incessant craving. The chasm those experiences created was difficult to breach. "Shall I drink it now?"

She shrugged with her hands, a small smile curving her lips, here and gone. "If you like."

I shot the liquid back. It tasted bitter, instantly coating the back of my throat. A sharp-sweet flavor chased the bitterness. I grimaced. "That is disgusting!"

"Don't make me tell you what's in it," she laughed. "I hope it will help."

"I'm sure it will." I set the empty bottle to the side, casting around for a glass of water, but I had none. Smacking my lips, I sat on the edge of my bed and invited Laura to join me.

Before I could say anything, Laura said, "I'm sorry I haven't visited more often."

Now the scratch at my throat had nothing to do with the vile potion. "You're the Queen. No doubt you have plenty of things to do. I do have a question, though."

Calyse had mentioned a secret that he had kept about Endymion for a hundred years. Now that Laura had married him, wouldn't she know what it was? I still didn't have a firm grasp on the threat Cal feared was in the castle, only that it had something to do with an enemy and eyes turning black.

Laura squared herself to face me, listening. Her golden eyes held mine.

"Last week, I told Calyse I saw a woman who had black eyes— all black, on the inside. He thinks there's some threat associated with her, but when he told the King, he... dismissed him." He dismissed me most of all, but I didn't add that.

"All black?" I could see her mind working.

"Yes. Do you know what he was afraid of, what this might have to do with an enemy in the castle? Calyse is still convinced there's a danger."

Contemplatively, she dropped her eyes to the palm of her hand, where darkness swirled. "We defeated him."

"That's what Endymion said."

She quirked her lips to the side, still not looking at me.

"What aren't you telling me?" I asked. With every second, the chasm between us only grew wider. "Is someone a danger to you or to me?"

"I hope not." She laced the dark shadows between her fingers.

"Some of the other women have seen them as well. The eyes."

She met my gaze again. Her breathing had grown shallower. "That's..." But she only chewed her lip.

"Laura," I insisted, "tell me. I'm your sister. I'll fight them off, remember?" We both knew I couldn't make good on that promise, but I would damn well try.

"Im Scathail," she said in an undertone. I'd heard the name before. Vaguely, I associated it with an evil force. "It's possible that part of him survived after..." Again, she flexed her hands. "You can't tell anyone."

"I won't." My heart beat faster. Finally, I would understand what was going on.

"When I arrived, Im Scathail had... possessed Endymion. His shadows used End's body to terrorize the palace for years. No one knew but Calyse and a couple others. To defeat the enemy, Endymion ordered that he be killed."

"Im Scathail?"

"Himself, because he couldn't separate the two."

My blood felt like ice. "But the King's alive."

"He wasn't. He died." Her eyes grew haunted, as though she were gazing at her husband's lifeless body.

Reality hit me like a slap. Calyse. Calyse must have killed him. Then how...?

"I don't know exactly what happened," Laura continued, her voice growing smaller. "I begged for his life, offered everything I had, and somehow... somehow the shadows entered me, but I could control them. You've seen it. I've never been overtaken like End was. But what if..."

My mind spun.

"What if some of them escaped?"

I clasped my sister's hands. If I understood the story, of everyone in the castle, she was in the most danger. Im Scathail, that faceless threat, would target her for using some of his power.

"What can I do?" I asked.

"Nothing. Hopefully it's nothing."

Her sudden switch to nonchalance pricked me with irritation. "It's obviously something. Did Endymion's eyes turn black when he was possessed?"

She looked at me almost bashfully. "In the worst moments. Was the person you saw covered in shadows?"

"What do you mean?"

"Did they seem to smoke, shadows surrounding them?"

"No. The woman looked normal except for the eyes." Ethereally gorgeous and carrying a bird, but otherwise normal.

"Will you tell me if you see anyone else?"

"Calyse is looking into it as well," I said. "He's very concerned. And I'm concerned. I want you to be safe."

She squeezed our linked hands. "Don't worry about me. I can defend myself now." She smiled. The implication, though, was that I couldn't, at least not by comparison. I chewed the inside of my lip.

"Turn around," I said, smoothing her long blonde hair through my fingers. This way, she wouldn't have to see the pain on my face. "I'll show you how to do the fishtail braid."

❦ 13 ❦

I took their lack of faith as a challenge.

I'd seen a woman with all-black eyes. If Calyse and Laura were correct, that meant that some vestige of the enemy Im Scathail had infiltrated the castle. I'd be damned before I let anything hurt Laura. Yes, she was stronger than I was now, but I was her older sister.

A nebulous plan had pieced itself together in my mind. I would rid the castle of this threat to her and then I would leave, whether that meant recovering enough to be released from constant surveillance or running away. I needed freedom and Laura didn't need the burden of looking after me. Besides, there was no more fairy fruit in the castle, but it undoubtedly existed somewhere outside it.

Calyse stood back at his post outside my room the next day. As I predicted, he looked tired, but he gave me a roguish smile when he saw me emerge.

"Good morning, Lizzie. You look well-rested and upset."

He was right. Laura's potion had allowed me to dream of

something other than finding the fruit I craved, but I awoke in a terrible mood.

I grunted at him.

"Would you like to hit me today?" he teased.

"No." I stopped. "I talked to Laura yesterday. I know about Im Scathail."

He scratched the back of his neck. "Don't speak loudly."

His command made me want to shout, but Laura had advised the same, that I should not tell anyone what I had learned. Calyse, however, had played a part in the dramatic events that led to my waking. "I want to protect her," I said simply. "There has to be more I can do than talking to the women."

He regarded me seriously. "I have thought—" He shook his head. "Never mind."

"What? Tell me." All this hesitation and secrecy was driving me mad.

"I wouldn't."

"Calyse," I hissed.

"I wouldn't." But what he wouldn't do, he didn't say.

"I'll do anything to help," I offered. "I'm not doing any good here otherwise."

His brows twitched downward, disagreeing. "You're doing enough as it is."

I wanted to push him. "Existing isn't enough for me. I want to help my sister."

A look of understanding deepened in his face. I thought of Laura's implication that *someone* had followed through on Endymion's command to kill him so the kingdom would be free of the enemy. My insides twisted, but whether from the feeling of being seen or the knowledge of what he had probably done, I couldn't say.

We stared at each other. Despite my body's slow recovery, my will was as strong as ever.

"Nemesis," he muttered. "I can't put you in danger."

"What do you mean? What could I do to help?"

"Lizzie." He placed his hands on my shoulders. "My job is to see you recover, not to put you in more peril. Your sister would take my head."

I took a calming breath, but it did little to placate my roiling feelings. His loyalty to Endymion and my sister was preventing me from helping them. Admiration and fury battled inside me.

"You want to get rid of this threat as much as I do." Lowering my voice, I added, "Think of all you've done already to get rid of it."

My guess was confirmed when his lips parted in surprise and his grip on my shoulders tightened. His wide eyes searched mine. "What do you know?" This was the commanding Calyse I'd seen in the tower. The warrior, not the friend.

"Laura told me," I lied.

"No one can know," he said, fierce but quiet.

"Just think," I said, matching his tone, "of all you're willing to do. Your sacrifices need to matter. Let me help."

He let his hands slip off my shoulders. His expression was so piercing that for a moment I thought he might kiss me. It was silly, perhaps, considering all the much more scandalous things we'd done, but my stomach flipped.

He swore, then gave a disbelieving laugh. "You're a menace. I'll think about it. I'll think about it."

That had to be enough for me. At least for now.

WITH LITTLE ELSE TO DO, I OFFERED TO FISH BRAID ALL THE women's hair at breakfast. Calyse kept looking at me as though I would storm away to seek out and destroy the bird woman myself. Honestly, I would have, if I'd had the slightest clue where to start.

Seeing smiles cross the women's faces as they admired each other's hair gave me a momentary reprieve from the yearning that had settled in my chest.

If it wasn't fairy fruit, I longed for freedom. If it wasn't freedom, I longed for Laura's safety. If it wasn't Laura's safety, I longed for the escape Calyse's body could give me.

I was a mass of cravings, and I feared I would never be satisfied.

Familiar malaise began to grip me midday, and the fantasy of plump cherries and ice-cold melon threaded compulsively through my thoughts. I drew my hands into fists, digging my nails into my palms.

Calyse, the ever-present watchman, eyed me with new concern. "Can I show you something? It's on the other side of the castle."

I felt weaker than usual, but refused to admit it. "What is it?"

"Why tell you when you can guess?" He smiled. "There's that glare I like."

Despite my annoyance, I was grateful for a distraction. He kept his pace moderate as we made our way through the castle. My cycling thoughts about fairy fruit hardly allowed me to see the soaring ceilings and magnificent sculptures. I scanned passing faces, absently looking for the beautiful bird woman, but didn't find her. Calyse's broad back bobbed in front of me for a long time. Periodically, he looked back to make sure I was right behind him. We passed through a huge arcade that felt familiar, though I couldn't remember why. He led us across the open space to a small descending staircase ending in a locked door. He produced a key and let us inside.

We stepped into a marble hallway dotted with metal sconces molded to look like animals. No one else was here. It was as though we had the floor to ourselves. Compared to above, the privacy was striking.

"What is this?" I asked.

His usually jovial face looked grim. "It's the lower level. No one is allowed down here. This is where you and the others slept."

My cheeks felt cold, and not only from the stony coolness of the air. I had no memory of waking up besides one vivid image of a room with rows of sheet-covered figures, like a mass tomb.

Calyse pointed to the left. "Your sister stayed over there." His orange eyes filled with painful memories.

"Why are you showing me this?" I whispered. It felt like a sacred space, somehow.

"If your sister trusts you enough to tell you what happened, then I must as well. This place..." He took a deep breath. "I still live down here."

The sudden shift jarred me. "What?"

"Right down there." He pointed right. We still stood just inside the door to the upper floor. It was as if he felt reluctant to go deeper.

How terrible to live in a place with such memories! I hated the East Wing, but I hadn't lived there for decades. I hadn't been commanded to kill my best friend.

I placed a comforting hand on his big shoulder. He smirked at it and started moving right down the hall. He rattled off what lay behind each door as we passed it. The sleeping maidens, a library...

Passages branched off from the main corridor. We swerved deeper into the maze of halls until—especially with my craving as heightened as it was today—I felt sure I couldn't get out alone. Finally, we reached an interior door with a handle carved like a badger, its nose worn to bronze. Calyse drew out a new key and opened it.

Weapons adorned the walls in a decorative pattern. Two chandeliers cast light over the gleaming metal and over the rest of the room, divided into two tiers. On a raised step sat a large bed three times the size of my small one, a wardrobe, and a fireplace. On the lower tier, a large chair sat before a huge cabinet of bottles and herbs and liquid substances. I had limited knowledge of potions, but knew enough to gather that all these ingredients and tools could manufacture a wide range of charms, hexes, and remedies. Beside the chair was a table filled with papers and scrolls—maps, for the most part—as well as wicked-looking metal instruments I associated with surgery. Finally, there was an inset pool near where the bed sat on the upper step. Its waters churned on their own, much like Endymion's had in his more luxurious version.

Calyse's solemn behavior as he stepped into his room prepared me to listen. Something weighed heavily on his mind, and it wasn't just the black eyes or his reassignment to observe me instead of doing what he really wanted. Something like apprehension settled in my belly, and also pride that he would show me this private space.

"This is it," he said, opening his arms, but he wasn't smiling. "This is why I don't want you to involve yourself with the Enemy."

## 14

Calyse's room provided no comfortable place to sit. He never hosted friends here. The realization saddened me. Besides the raised bed or the ominous chair set in front of the apothecary cabinet, I could see nowhere to settle as he talked.

"We tried everything when End was... overtaken," he said, his gaze darting to the shelves of bottles, to the metal instruments. "Everything. We sought out every remedy. I traveled to the far reaches with him only to watch him suffer. No matter what I did, his suffering continued." His lashes fluttered with painful memory. "I know he's a stubborn bastard, but he's my best friend. And I watched him suffer again and again and again. Always a secret. That's why he built this area. So we could find some way to cure him and so... no one could hear him screaming."

He collected himself and met my eyes once more. "The Enemy doesn't merely kill. It destroys, and it uses others to destroy." His shoulders flexed. "The palace will never know what we endured, and it cannot. If there is a chance that anything of the kind could happen again, I'd give body and soul to stop it. So," he said, "I will eliminate the threat without you."

"But—"

"I won't go through that again."

Despairingly, I looked once more at the collection of potions. His urgency to get to Endymion made more sense now. My heart ached for what Calyse had endured. To watch his best friend suffer year after year... Imagining something similar happening to Laura brought tears to my eyes. How did Calyse manage to smile so often?

What if Calyse got possessed next?

I felt sick. "You can't do it alone," I said.

"I won't do it with you."

"You have no choice. You have to bring me everywhere."

He laughed drily.

We stood close now, at odds yet allied in our determination not to let this threat hurt the ones we loved. Honest concern for me showed in his handsome face.

I licked my dry lips, hoping he understood that I too would give anything.

In that quiet moment, the air shifted. Fearful vulnerability threatened to drown me. Not only did I want Calyse, but I admired him. I liked him. Deeply. And I didn't want to.

His gaze smoldered with the same emotion, his heartbeat ticking visibly in his throat. Slowly, tentatively, he leaned close until we were almost touching. Heat spread from my neck to my chest and down. His breath feathered across my face.

This was different than the other times. Unplanned, and more than a fun distraction. This time could magnify my vulnerability and my hurt. This time could leave me devastated.

I stepped back.

The heat building between us dissipated. I exhaled, trying to hide how much I was trembling.

"Oh," he said, breathless, "not today. That's fine." But I could tell he was shaken. "All this gloomy talk doesn't exactly make you want to jump in bed, does it?" He reached for a smile and barely managed one.

"No," I said, though my voice sounded equally husky.

He cleared his throat. "So you can see why I want to keep you out of everything. The risk is too great."

It was no use arguing, so I didn't. But I also didn't plan to stand by while my sister was in danger. I simply wasn't sure how to help her yet.

"You seem to be having a difficult day today," he said, his demeanor changing altogether.

I didn't want to admit it. My problems sounded small in light of the century of torture he'd just described.

"It doesn't matter."

"So am I, if I'm honest. Tell me about Selene."

I nearly choked. "It's boring compared to this."

"I've never been over the barrier, but I've imagined what it's like." His eyes went almost dreamy.

I felt my face relax, the precursor to a smile. "What did you imagine?"

His expression sharpened again and he eyed me. This was a plan to cheer me up. That, or he was about to say something terrible. "Poor, helpless humans surrounded by packs of wolves. The strongest warriors would go out to face them, of course, but the rest would try to comfort each other inside."

His tone held such condescension that I smacked him.

He laughed. "Or sometimes, I picture societies of people creating books—like your sister does—and cultivating gardens and considering the universe." He leveled his gaze at me. "The problem is that they only have part of the picture. And so do we."

I couldn't help being drawn to this deeper part of him. On the surface he was all muscle and humor, but inside he thought about bigger questions and fought ruthlessly for his friends.

I replied a beat too late. "Those are only half true. I'm sure if you met all of us, we wouldn't seem worthy of all your imaginings."

"After all these years, you can't stop me from thinking about it. Set my thoughts in order, then. What is it like?"

Images of my life in Selene played out before my mind—all the women of our household sitting in front of the fire so we didn't freeze in winter, Laura and I going to a dance in a barn, the smell of the bookbinder's, James the baker asking for my hand in marriage... "It's almost easier to start with what it's not."

He raised his eyebrows encouragingly.

"It's not wild; it's contained. There's still blood and..." My throat constricted as I gestured lamely to mean *sex*. "But it's behind closed doors. No one talks about it unless they're referencing you. The Fae. The forest creatures. It's all caution and survival." I trailed off, wondering if I was wrong not to remember my village in better terms.

"Wolves?"

Calyse's voice snapped me out of my reverie.

"Not often!" I laughed. "I wanted to be free of it all. I just didn't want to end up like this." Confessing the truth felt like releasing air from a balloon that had only expanded wider and wider in my chest.

When Calyse looked at me expectantly, keeping any more snarky comments to himself, I forged on. "Women don't have much sway in Selene. So many of us were taken." I set my jaw. I'd been taken too. No matter how many times I reminded myself that that part wasn't my fault, shame, piercing and hot, still washed over me whenever I remembered.

Running my hands over the apothecary bottles so I didn't have to look at Calyse, I said, "I didn't want to settle down and have a family, but that just made me wrong. No other woman was like me, wanting travel and play and... to be my own person, without another name attached." I swallowed the hard knot in my throat. "Maybe I was broken then too." Until that moment, I hadn't realized how much I wanted either to be accepted fully or to change. The tension of always having people look at me as the odd one, the wild one, but knowing that's what I wanted anyway pulled my heart taut as a slingshot with nowhere to aim.

"You're not broken," came Calyse's low voice, made lower with emotion and conviction.

I turned to face him. Lines crisscrossed his forehead, deepening the shadows cast over his eyes. As if the veneer of bravado had been ripped away, he stood exposed. He wanted me to believe him, and I wished I could.

"How do you know?" I challenged. "You barely know me. To you, I'm just like a leaf that's here one season and then gone."

His breathing sped up. "I know because I've met so many people. Here among the Fae, at least, it's common to let life pass over you, reacting only if something floats by like leaves on a river."

A concession to my analogy. I'd never heard Calyse sound so poetic.

"You and your sister don't do that. You both had every reason to be afraid, but you still try to do courageous things for each other and even for us." He canted his head slight, knowing. "If anything, that's cracked, not broken."

Stupid Calyse, making me fall in love with him.

"I could play the flute for you to cheer you up." His mischievous smirk returned. "End never lets me play for him."

I wished he had said something else, maybe ordered me back to the East Wing or shown me the place where I'd lain asleep for months. Something I could dislike. Instead, I silently cursed his charm.

"Fine," I sighed.

His expression of absolute delight made me furiously happy.

## 15

Georgina and I sucked on lemon sweets offered by a squirrel boy. She made little sounds of pleasure as she ate. It was nice to see her enjoying anything, since she usually acted so distant.

After hearing Calyse play the flute in his chambers, I felt revived enough to take another evening walk. It wasn't lost on me that now I was searching for distractions from my distraction. Whatever had passed between us in his room still buzzed under my skin. I tried not to look at him. Our situation had not changed. He was still my jailer and I was still his prisoner, even though he didn't see it that way.

Georgina looked at me with a clearer expression than I'd ever seen on her. "The cottage where my son lives, it's the one with the garden behind it, and the paddock for horses?"

"That's the one," I confirmed. Laura and I had talked about living there ourselves and becoming little old ladies together.

"We could never manage a place so grand when he was a child." Moisture rimmed the inside of her eyes. She took refuge in the sweet.

"I assure you, it's true. He's there with his entire family." I didn't know if the sheriff was happy, but his situation certainly caused envy among the others in Selene.

"I wish I could see him." Her tone took on that distant quality again.

Once, I remembered going to the barrier that sliced down the edge of the forest. The magic was invisible. Theoretically, Georgina could see her son again if I could set up a meeting somehow. Tasting fairy fruit prevented us from passing through the barrier, but why not go to the edge?

I spun to address Calyse, quietly following us like a gigantic shadow. "Is there anyone here who can pass through the barrier? Forest creatures?"

He thought for a moment before shaking his head. "The kingdoms are separate," he said.

"No one?" That seemed impossible. How could so many beings dwell in the same world and be unable to contact each other.

To solve this riddle was easier than clearing the castle of the shadowy Im Scathail. Besides, if I could figure out how to let Georgina reunite with her son, that meant that I might be able to see Mother again too.

Freedom meant home. It meant more than that, but home had always been part of it. I just hadn't realized that until now.

"Animals can move back and forth," Calyse continued, "and humans. But humans usually don't make it very far."

I clamped my teeth. All the stories I heard growing up about not only lost maidens but also distraught husbands or lovers who charged in after them never included anyone returning to the village. To pass the barrier for more than a dareful moment meant death or, as I had discovered, captivity.

A scream sliced through my thoughts.

Georgina and I were only a few minutes from the East Wing now, almost within sight of it, and the scream had certainly come from that direction. The lemon sweet turned to ash in my mouth. What was wrong?

Calyse sprinted ahead of us to find out. I picked up my pace as well. Even Georgina hurried as much as she was able.

Women of Selene, most still in their white sleeping gowns, overflowed from the main area where we took our meals. They all faced inward, staring at something. Calyse's voice rose above the cries, the whimpers, the whispered curses of horror, which were growing louder.

"What happened?" he demanded. "Who did this? Back away!"

None of the voices could answer him.

I finally approached near enough to see through the crowd of heads. Immediately, I wished I hadn't.

Laid out on the long wooden table was the eviscerated body of Eve, whom I had just spoken to a few days before. I wouldn't have recognized her without the white streaks in her hair. The back of my throat lunged up. Blood pooled black around her body, dripping off the edge of the table, but the worst part was her injury. She'd been cut vertically down the center until she lay almost in half.

I backed away, fighting back sickness. Just enough presence of mind remained that I was able to take Georgina firmly by the shoulders and turn her around before she saw the corpse.

Calyse was trying to calm the women down and get answers. Eve never could have done something so heinous to herself. Someone strong had murdered her and laid her out as a message.

"What happened?" Georgina asked, the lemon sweet forgotten in her hand.

"Just come over here," I managed, guiding her farther away. Calyse would be looking for me, so I stayed within sight of him while he addressed the scene. Luckily, he was taller than the women, so I was still shielded from the hideous sight.

The noises of shocked women, already so traumatized from their long comas, and Calyse's commanding voice blended into a wave of horror. I didn't know how long I stood there, unmoving, with Georgina, who had the good sense to follow my example. Vomit kept threatening to rise up and choke me.

"Lizzie!" The cry seemed to come from far away. But then arms embraced me in a fierce hug, nearly knocking me over. "Lizzie, you're all right!" Wetness coated my shoulder and I realized Laura was crying.

Endymion had come too. A line furrowed between his dark brows.

Calyse rushed over to us. "It's a woman. Dead," he reported. "There's an immense amount of blood. She was sliced clean through. End." He grew more intense as he stared at his friend. "You know what this could mean."

A muscle ticked in Endymion's jaw. "Find out what happened." The low, cultured voice of the King brooked no opposition.

"I think we know what happened." Fire blazed in Calyse's eyes.

The King only repeated, "Find out."

Laura still hadn't released me from our hug. She stroked my hair, my back that hitched unevenly even though no tears fell. "You'll stay somewhere away from here tonight," she said quietly in my ear.

I didn't protest as she led me away. Dimly, I saw that Georgina was being led away from the East Wing too. None of us would have to sleep in that cursed place tonight.

Endymion stayed behind to confer with Calyse.

Together, Laura and I trundled down the paths of the castle. She wrapped one arm around my waist, while her shadows writhed inside her open other hand in case of danger. I didn't speak.

Only a couple minutes later, she opened yet another new area of the castle, this one a room lush with moss and greenery, the kind of room that would have enchanted us as children. A mound I'd mistaken for a mossy stone actually turned out to be a bed. It wasn't large. Perhaps this room really was for children. Silently, the two of us curled under the covers. Laura held me tight. Her familiar warmth calmed me, but her breathing had become deep and slow long before I found any rest.

## 16

What happened to Eve? Did it have anything to do with Calyse's fears about the Enemy in our midst? His reaction suggested that it did.

Even if Im Scathail had nothing to do with the horrifying murder, someone had killed the woman in a way that threatened the rest of us too.

How could I protect Laura if I couldn't protect myself?

We'd switched positions in the night. I now held her, just as we used to in our shared bed. Her familiar scent, like soap and oranges, slowed my heartbeat but not my racing thoughts. I wanted to hold her here forever.

Long ago—it felt like long ago—we were everything to one another. I'd given up my future to make her life secure. Surely, there was more I could do to keep her safe from this threat than merely to somehow recover from my obsessive cravings. I tightened my arms around her and kissed the back of her head.

In this moment, I told myself, I wasn't helpless.

In this moment, I was the sister Laura needed.

She stirred in her sleep. I buried my head deeper into the

mossy pillow, scowling against the inevitable morning and the parting that would come with it.

Did Calyse know where I was?

The knowledge that his watch over me would resume as soon as we left this room left me more comforted than it should have. I wanted to see him, to talk to him about what had happened.

Laura rolled over, scooching to face me. I gazed at her, trying to pour all my feelings in the past few months into the silence between us. She understood—some of it, at least—because she snuggled up next to me again and said, "Not yet."

❦

EVENTUALLY, LAURA LEFT WITH ENDYMION, AND I WENT WITH Calyse back to the private lower level of the castle, this time to a dining room. Though sumptuous food filled the table, neither of us reached for anything.

Although he had changed out of his leathers into other clothes, Calyse clearly hadn't slept at all. His eyes, already deep-set and dark, looked bruised. The signature smile he usually wore was missing. I wanted to take his hand, but kept my fists in my lap.

"Did you find out who did it?" I asked.

"No," he said bitterly. "I know who did it, but I don't know who he used."

"Is there a reason he chose her?"

"Blood. He just needed her blood."

I shuddered, chills covering my body. That revelation felt worse than knowing Eve had been specifically targeted. That gruesome murder could have happened to any of us.

"Why?"

"It's a key to all black magic. It gives him power, strength..."

He pounded the table with his fist so hard the dishes clinked together. One glass toppled and broke.

I jumped.

He crumpled forward, his head in his hands. Thick strands of hair fell forward. His back rose and fell in deep, measured breaths, almost as if he were counting them out, before he straightened again. As he scanned the table, his jaw worked.

He wanted nothing more than to end this threat to us all, but instead he was here with me.

Today, I wouldn't do anything rash. I wouldn't put myself in danger or run away or try to track down fairy fruit. Today, I would do whatever Calyse needed from me.

I uncurled my hands and placed them on the table, available. "What do you want me to do? I'll stay down here if it will help." That wasn't what I wanted, but the anguish in Calyse's eyes dug like a knife into my chest.

"It might." The words came out flat, almost lifeless.

"All right, then I will."

He seemed to remember I sat beside him because he focused on me, one brow slightly quirked. "No battle from my nemesis today?" A smile still didn't appear, but the comment nudged close to teasing, so I felt satisfied I'd done something right.

"Not today," I answered. "Maybe tomorrow."

His face relaxed. The quality of his look took me back to that moment in his room. There was gratefulness, but more than that. In some indefinable way, he *saw* me.

"Are the rest of the women all right?" I asked.

"They've been housed separately in new locations."

"Good."

"I need to talk to them all." He rose from his chair and wavered, actually wavered on his feet. It was slight, but for such a mountainous figure, even that much movement was obvious.

I shot to my feet. "You can do it in a few hours," I proclaimed, looping my arm around his waist as Laura had done for me last night. "You haven't slept in a few days. Don't lie and say you have."

He glared at me but let me lead him out of the dining room.

"You're a frustrating human, you know."

"I know. Where's your room?"

He growled under his breath but pointed the way through the winding corridors. When I saw the badger door handle, I knew we'd arrived.

"Key," I said.

He gave me a pointed look, but opened the lock himself. "I can't sleep long," he said, going inside.

I disentangled my arm from his waist. He wasn't wobbling anymore, but I still saw the heavy slope of his shoulders and the black around his eyes.

"I'll stand guard," I teased.

"More likely you'll run off," he muttered, though relief finally shone through his features. "You're not coming inside?"

I froze.

"We don't have to do anything," he explained, "but I have a bath, and the bed is large enough for you to have your own side. Or I have a few books."

All of that sounded far preferable to staying out in the cold corridor. "It's mid-morning. What happened to 'sleep short'?"

"Sleep was your idea," he reminded me, shucking off his shirt and throwing it to the side of the lofted bed.

I couldn't think of a witty retort. All I could focus on was that skin I wanted to touch and the Fae beneath that I wanted to comfort.

He toed off his boots and let them clatter to the floor.

My eyes darted to the churning pool, to the books scattered

among the maps on the table, then back to the big bed. Its smooth sheets were deep blue, the color of early night when fireflies rose from the grasses.

With a sigh, partly from frustration and partly from relief, Calyse climbed in bed. "Make yourself comfortable," he called. "And wake me in a couple hours. Don't let me sleep longer."

I hadn't moved from the door.

"Or you can come up here," he said, teasing and blurry with exhaustion. His eyes had already closed.

I made up my mind. Marching to the bed, I kicked off my own shoes but left my dress on before sliding between the sheets.

He opened his eyes, a little surprised. Only half of his face was visible above the deep pillow. I settled next to him.

"I want to hold you," I murmured. As I wrapped myself around him, I tried to make it clear that I didn't want anything more from him. He was too tired and I didn't know what it might mean if we did have sex again. It wouldn't be the same as the previous times. I knew that much.

He allowed me to embrace him with my head resting against his firm chest. This time, when he sighed, I sensed no frustration. His hands came up to hold me in place, linking behind my back. I felt his heart beat slow and steady under my ear.

A new sort of ache twisted in my chest as I listened to him fall asleep.

## 17

The next morning, after waking up in bed with Calyse, his warm face nestled against my hair, we set to work planning how to snare the Shadow.

Im Scathail had used Eve's blood as an ingredient for dark magic. Time was running out before the enemy would become stronger and threaten Laura, Endymion, and the rest of us. All of them had already gone through enough trying to defeat this ancient evil. It was time to end it once and for all.

As much as I wanted to stay in bed, feeling the musculature of Calyse's chest and sampling his amber-smoke kisses, we had a job. Besides, the feelings budding inside my ribcage for him frightened me.

We sat together at the edge of the bed. The sheets beckoned me back. I rubbed my eyes and banished the thought. Calyse looked softer after sleep, not the living weapon he usually seemed.

"We don't know where the possessed Fae are," he said, voice throaty with sleep.

My stomach tugged at the noise.

"But I can think of a way to lure them. It's not how I wanted to do it, but we have to finish this goddamn villain before he spreads." His jaw hardened. He wasn't looking at me.

I tried to catch his eyeline. Finally, he relented. Fire blazed in his eyes, but not the kind I'd seen in the tower. It was a new kind of ferocity.

"You need me," I guessed.

"It would speed up the hunt." He blew out a breath. "If anyone touches you, I swear I'll kill them."

A pleasant shiver raced down my back. "What do I have to do?"

"You don't *have* to do anything. I hate that this is the only idea I have to catch this monster..." He leaned his meaty forearms on his knees.

"I want to. You were the one who said I couldn't get involved."

He grunted. "You need to stop remembering everything I say," he said with a smirk.

"So...?"

"So, the woman with the bird approached you at a party, led you to fairy fruit."

Even the mention of my craving snagged my mind hard. I struggled to focus on what he said next, my thoughts fixated on the juice, the flavors, the bliss...

"We get you alone again. Last time, the Shadow sought you out. Maybe he would do so a second time. Maybe there's a reason he chose you."

My core tightened with nerves. "Okay," I said. "Where? Another party?"

"We can try that first." He laid a hand over mine. "I'll be right there."

"While I'm alone? Doesn't that defeat your aim?"

"Out of sight," he said, exasperated. "You're always twisting my words."

"Or something else," I said before I could stop myself.

He smiled languorously, narrowing his eyes at me. "Oh ho! Not now when I have to focus, little nemesis."

I swallowed. "So, a party."

"Yes. If you are willing, ask for fairy fruit, just like before."

"But there's none in the castle." I needed to hear it aloud. But what if it wasn't true? What if there was still some hidden away in this huge palace? What if I got what I asked for? My desires pulled painfully in opposite directions.

"No, but your request got his attention last time. Recreating the situation might make him reveal himself."

Despite the fact that we'd just woken up, it was evening, a time rife with pleasure-seeking throughout the castle. There was probably a revel happening right now. I looked down at my dress. It was crumpled from sleeping.

"Then let's do it right away. Do I look all right for a party?" I stood in front of him. Even seated, he looked me in the face.

He raked his gaze over me. I hadn't been looking for a compliment—it had been a sincere question—but all I saw was hungry appreciation. "Don't ask me that," he said.

"Really, though, I won't stand out?"

"You'll always stand out. You're human."

"I mean, do I need a different dress?"

"You want me to take that one off you?"

My throat went dry as sand. Our dirty banter didn't feel as frivolous as it had. Not only my body reacted, but my emotions as well. I yearned to say yes, but instead I coughed once and said, "I'll just wear this one, then."

If he was disappointed, he didn't show it. He rose and thrust a knife into his belt before putting on his leather shirt. I helped him do the clasps in the back, remembering how it felt to undo them instead. My fingertips brushed the skin on his shoulders as I hooked the armor on. Goosebumps rippled wherever I touched him.

That done, he turned and wrapped his hair in a knot.

"I'll speak to a few others so they can go to the party as well," he said, his soldier persona in place.

"All right." My clashing desires left me almost dizzy. Above them all sounded the call to protect the castle and all its inhabitants from this threat. Their lives mattered more than my desire to lose myself in skin and pleasure.

"In an hour, I'll take you to the Den."

"The Den?"

But Calyse only gave one of his maddening smiles in answer.

❧

"EXCUSE ME," I SAID TO TWO HALF-BURNED FAE MALES sprawled over one another in the walkway. At least I assumed it was a walkway. The party Calyse had suggested before was nothing like this one, which had clearly been going on all day, if not all week. Fae and forest creatures, many completely unclothed, walked or danced or kissed or fucked. Some wore masks to hide their identities or add to the mystery. Others lounged on low settees while others poured red wine in their mouths. The very atmosphere felt awash with wine and sweat, instantly intoxicating.

Even for my wilder sensibilities, this place made me uncertain. Blood heated my cheeks. With so many bodies pressed together, it would have felt hot even without my blush. The music of pipes and drums thrummed low in my gut, beckoning me to undulate with it.

Someone gave a delighted scream.

I scanned the room for Calyse. He said he would look out for me while I made myself bait for the black-eyed woman. I even searched the higher platforms floating above this seething mass of sensual excess. Grass topped the upper levels and coated the ground here too, as though we were in a fantasy version of the forest. On the platforms, all I could see were glimpses of naked Fae women, but not Calyse's distinctive form. He had said something about bringing other warriors too. Since all Fae had stunning physiques, I couldn't be sure who were soldiers in disguise.

A tail wrapped sinuously around my ankles. I turned around sharply to find a forest creature with little horns peeking out of his brown curls and mostly human facial features, apart from his large, liquid eyes. They were strange, but animal, not the all-black hue I was looking for. "Sit with us, human," he purred.

Behind me, someone collided with my back. I looked to see a Fae couple locked in an amorous kiss, jostling those near me.

"No," I said thickly, trying to keep my head. "Do you... do you have fairy fruit?"

I tried hourly to keep that question from my thoughts. Voicing my desire aloud felt as scandalous as the female Fae whimpering as she was bent over the table of pitchers.

I tore my eyes away, back to the creature whose tail hadn't stopped caressing my leg.

"Fairy fruit?" His inquiring smile revealed sharp teeth. "I might be able to get you some. Come, come."

In a trance, I followed, brushing past a muscular male Fae carrying another on his shoulders so the higher one could kiss one of the women on the lowest platform.

After threading through so many beautiful bodies I felt short of breath and foggy-headed, we reached the side of the room, where various forest creatures arrayed themselves on a collection of stumps.

The sight reminded me so powerfully of entering the forest

that first time that I physically ached. There was a similar female that resembled an owl. There was a slim, weasel-like creature. None stood as tall as the Fae, but they were magnificent like the woods were magnificent, rustic like blood and water and soil. Many hands pulled me down to sit with them, to recline in their laps. I obeyed their urging.

My mouth had gone bitter. Where was the fairy fruit? Somewhere in the back of my mind was the thought that I was here for more than finding the fruit, but I couldn't remember what was more important.

The soft tail never stopped rubbing against my leg. It was his body I leaned against. "Where is it?" I asked.

"Relax," someone else hissed suggestively.

I tried, but I couldn't fully settle. Nailed fingers stroked the line where my neck and shoulder joined.

"I need it," I said.

"In time."

The music wormed its way into my body, encouraging me to take all earthly delights. Chief of which was the fruit.

With a mighty effort, I disentangled myself from the forest creatures and stood. "I'll find it myself," I said, my mission coming almost into focus in my mind.

Someone needed to offer it to me. That person would be evil.

I didn't fit into this wanton revel. I was human. I was broken.

Feeling small and fragile, I made my way faintly back in the direction I had come. Where was Calyse? He would know how to cheer me, or at least give me an outlet for the anger I felt at my situation.

Someone snagged my hand. It was a fully naked female Fae. She looked utterly unashamed of her curvy body. Lustrous hair fell almost to her breasts. A coy smile curved her lips when she caught me staring.

"Dance with me," she said.

What kind of dance could we do together, this naked woman and I? I had no idea what to say.

I stood still, but she sauntered close to me, her sensuous hips rolling with the movement. I'd never considered this sort of interaction before. The hand she held grew clammy. I watched her with curiosity and confusion. Why me?

She seemed amused by my dumbfounded expression, because she laughed right as she pressed herself against me. I felt all the curves of her body, which rocked against me to the beat.

"I've always wanted a mortal girl," she said, hoarse and low.

My eyes widened. "I don't know—"

She placed a finger over my lips. "Just try it."

I tried to relax, to move as she was moving, but something felt all wrong. It wasn't the luxurious press of her breasts against mine or the fingers she trailed at my hip, it was the sense I should be somewhere else.

Doing something else.

With someone else.

"Excuse me, I—" When I took a step back, her eyes had gone dark.

Black.

Something sprayed in my eye and across my mouth. I spit compulsively and stumbled backward. When I could open my eyes again, a broad circle had opened among the dancers and in the middle stood Calyse over the halved corpse of the naked woman.

❦ 18 ❦

The bird woman.

I hadn't recognized her without her pet.

Calyse's knife dripped with gore. In the dim light, it took me a moment to realize that shadows smoked from the woman in grasping tendrils.

He heaved in breath, more from ferocious anger than exertion. I saw it in his blazing eyes.

To my surprise, after the initial horror, the partygoers mostly resumed their activities. A few fled, others asked questions, still more helped remove the body.

Calyse strode forward, finding me in an empty pocket among the bodies, standing stock still. I didn't know whether to feel triumphant or sickened or simply to scream because my craving was roaring and I couldn't silence it.

My whole body trembled.

"That was a good job, Lizzie," he said with a tender note to his voice.

"No," I said, surprised that it came out as a sob.

He stepped closer, shielding me from anyone else who might

overhear. "I'm sorry you had to see that. Justice here can be quick and bloody. But I saw her eyes. You see, I always believed you. She had the Shadow in her."

"I know," I gasped, but I felt like I knew nothing at all. "It's this place. It's me. Arghhh!" My frustration came out as a growl. "I want... fruit." I hung my head as though I'd confessed to the greatest sin.

Calyse's bloody knife hung at his belt. Why could I not stop thinking of myself when Calyse had just murdered someone to stop the Enemy? I should make sure he was all right. I should mourn the loss of the person who had been someone before she was possessed. I should rejoice that my sister was out of danger. Everyone else was more important than I was right now.

"I'm sorry. I'm just"—my bitter-tasting throat worked—"broken."

"You're healing." He dragged his big arm around my shoulders and guided me to the entrance. I let myself lean against him, keeping my eyes closed.

I hated myself for asking, but I would have gone mad if I didn't. "Do you know where they took it all? If there's any left?"

"I wouldn't tell you if I did," he said gently. This wasn't the cavalier warrior, the seductive partner, or the fierce fighter. This was Calyse, my friend.

I squeezed my eyes tighter shut, disappointment in everything roiling deep inside me. I felt like I would drown.

"There's still more to do to clear the castle," he said, "but not tonight." He nudged me with his hip as we walked. "I told you those Fae parties were nothing like human ones."

I dug my face into his side.

He fell quiet. I focused on the rhythm of his walking, which he slowed to match my pace. It was childish to think I could shut out the world simply by closing my eyes, but I did it anyway.

"Stairs," he murmured, slowing so we could descend. The air cooled around us. My flushed face welcomed the underground chill.

We wove through the marble hallways until we halted in a dark space where no orange light pressed against my eyelids. The scraping of a key in a lock, and I knew we'd arrived back in Calyse's room.

I didn't want him to let go of me. His arm around me hushed the insistent repetition of my hungry craving. I could almost pretend I didn't long for it now, wouldn't lie or steal to get it. Almost.

The door closed behind us. As I had feared he would, he released me.

I slumped to the floor, my back against the wall, with my face in my hands. I couldn't face the world yet. Not yet.

Only a few seconds had passed before I felt Calyse lift me up, cradling me in his arms. I took in his smoky scent, mixed with some of the heady sweetness of the party's wine.

"What can I do?" I felt the question rumble in his chest.

"I don't know." What he was doing felt good enough.

"I'm going to put you on the bed."

I nodded. The silk covers rose to envelop me.

"Talk to me," he said.

I opened my eyes to see him unbuckling his knife belt before he sat beside me.

"There's nothing to say. I'm sorry I'm so selfish. I'm sorry I couldn't do more. I'm sorry I want the things I do."

"Lizzie." A hint of a chuckle laced the way he said my name. He met my burning eyes. "You are bad at one thing. Two, if you count sparring."

I sat up, shocked.

"You can't see yourself at all. You were willing to put yourself in danger to draw out the Shadow—which worked suspiciously well. You followed exactly the instruction I gave you, and also managed to give me a show that will haunt my dirtiest dreams. And you can't help what you want. You're doing everything you can to heal." He hooked a finger under my chin. "You are the most dangerous nemesis I could have because you're as fierce as any Fae, strong as stone, and naughty as an escaped rabbit." His eyes became hooded in his blood-flecked face. "I wake up wondering what you'll say. I dream of ways to pleasure you. And I hope that something I'm doing helps you win this battle you're fighting against yourself."

Tears stood in my eyes. "Calyse..."

"Say my name again."

"Calyse." My chest heaved, but not with old desires. With new ones. "Calyse."

He moaned.

"Calyse. Treat me like I'm not broken. I want you. I want you to take me." Before I'd finished speaking, he'd swept me in his arms, sending me backwards against the mattress. His mouth found mine, hungry and wanting.

This kiss was new. It was honest.

As always, he was careful not to lower his entire weight on me so I arched to meet him, opening my mouth so he could taste all of me, even the bitter, broken parts. He swept his tongue inside. I licked it and then I closed my mouth and sucked hard.

He growled, sliding his tongue out of my mouth before crushing his lips to mine again. "Dirty girl."

"You like it that way."

"You know me too well."

My legs wrapped around and gripped his hips. I toed off my shoes and flung them somewhere. In answer, he rolled against me, teasing my core, which grew more and more sensitive each time he moved.

We stayed like that for a while, my skin aching for more of him as our mouths moved. I nipped at his lip.

He smirked at me, giving my neck a soft bite.

I smirked back, grazing a generous muscle on his chest with my teeth.

"Harder," he said.

I obliged, earning a shudder. When I found his eyeline again, I gazed seriously at him. "Do everything you've wanted to do to me."

His breath halted for a beat. I felt the bulge in his pants grow bigger, harder. "You don't... You can't mean that."

"I doubt you'll be too rough for me."

"Fuck it, you do remember everything I say." He tried to laugh but was failing. It wasn't common to see a flustered Fae.

"I... trust you," I said, then lowered my voice to a whisper. "And I think I'll like it. Because I like you. Perhaps more than anyone before." The truth was stronger than that, but the final words took courage. Summoning it, I finished with the truth. "Calyse."

The eyes in his blood-speckled face were as wide as if I had suddenly struck him.

"I love you."

## 19

"**D**on't say that."

Calyse's reaction to my confession stunned me. I scooched up from underneath him to sit against the headboard. "What?"

He sat back on his knees with a grimace. His trousers fit too tightly over his erection. "I mean, do not say that to me if you don't intend every word. I've barely been keeping myself in check these past few—"

"This is you keeping yourself in check?" My comment came out rude. His apparent dismissal of my words stung deeply. I thought that perhaps the Fae warrior loved me. Even as I thought it now, the idea sounded ludicrous.

"Yes." His brow furrowed as he looked at me. "Listen. I didn't expect to become obsessed with you. For a hundred years, I've known little but pain. Don't say you love me for a good fuck. Say it because..." He stopped, out of breath.

"I love you," I said, stronger, slower. In all his raving, he hadn't said the words back to me. Perhaps it was foolish of me to want them, even after all this talk of obsession, but I did.

I waited, not moving toward him. The entire room seemed to crackle with the force building between us, hot and sharp. His every muscle flexed.

"Lizzie." My name fell off his tongue like warm syrup. He tasted every syllable. "I love—"

He didn't get the final word out before I kissed him, surging against him to touch him everywhere. "I'm not human," he grated with the last of his self-control. "Tell me to stop or else I won't."

"Don't stop," I begged. "Do everything."

With a growl that was more like a roar, he ripped my dress down the front, exposing me to him. He took the front of one breast in his mouth. I felt his teeth almost break the skin.

He was feral, and I liked it.

"Damn this!" he cried, reaching behind him to undo the leather armor.

I reached around him for the clasps and unhooked them as quickly as I could, desperate to feel his skin against mine. He threw away his clothes with disgust, as though they'd offended him. He grabbed the rags of the dress still around my hips and flung them in the pile. Only my underwear remained.

"You infuriating, maddening, little nemesis," he muttered as though in a trace. He saw through the haze of his lust long enough to wink at me.

He licked my face roughly, and I realized he was tasting the spray of blood. My heart thundered.

"Bad," I said, but the word was a breath. My lust-soaked senses could focus on nothing but the places our bodies touched and places we weren't touching. I reached for him with my own tongue, found his, tasted copper.

He grunted in response, kissing me so hard I felt drowned in pillows. He pushed me down with one motion of his big body over mine.

"I want... all of you..." he growled in my ear before licking my earlobe.

Before I could register what he was doing, he had torn off the band in his hair, freeing the locks to fall wild around his face, and used it to bind my wrists together as he'd done to himself in my room. I cried out as he pinned my arms up above my head and secured them there.

I whimpered, needing him to touch my hard nipples, my pulsing clit, needing him inside me. The landscape of his abs and his stiff cock beneath made me helpless with need.

He rolled his hips twice against me, teasing. His laugh was evil and wild. I writhed in my bonds, loving and hating not being able to touch him. Why were we always begging?

He licked my face once again before making his way down my body, biting and kissing and sucking, investigating the underside of my breast, my ribs, my navel. Finally, he took the seam of my underwear in his teeth and pulled it off. He tugged me toward him slightly, so my arms stretched just into pain, before settling himself down between my legs.

"Ah! Oh... oh, oh yes!" The praise burst out of me as I squirmed against his mouth. His tongue and fingers and teeth worked together. He licked savagely, relentlessly, right where I needed him. As though I were fairy fruit itself, he sucked on me, flicking his tongue between my folds.

I bucked against him, but every time I moved or my muscles contracted around him, the bonds cut into my wrists. The pain only heightened the sweet sensation in my core. Calyse knew it. He knew just how far to pull, just where to pulse his tongue.

A scream built deep in my belly. I knew he was watching me, seeing if I would break. He wrapped his arms around my thighs, pressing my core to him and stretching me just a little further. As he buried his face in me again, I screamed.

Shuddering violently, I felt the pressure against my wrists relax as Calyse pushed me forward again, a grin on his wet mouth. I twisted my bonds, but he just shook his head wickedly and kissed me. "Not yet."

I bared my teeth at him. His dark eyes sparkled with savage glee.

"Open," he said.

I did.

On his knees, he straddled me and fit his swollen dick into my mouth. He slid in slowly, testing, until he hit the back of my throat. I would choke if he tried to stuff himself in completely. He went carefully again one more time, judging the depth, before he gripped the top of the headboard, released a euphoric moan, and started thrusting.

I rubbed my tongue against the firm underside.

"Oh!" In front of me, his lower half tensed, trembling.

I did it again.

"God, Lizzie." The words were gasps, half panted air. "Suck. That's... Yes. Now teeth. Scrape... Oh, oh, oh, oh God! Do it again like that."

As if he couldn't help himself, he pressed in farther than he had. I coughed when he came out.

"Enough... of that. I'm sorry." He sat back on his heels, his cock hard as a pipe.

I licked my lips. "But you're not finished with me."

"Oh." A wide smile split his face. He bit down on his generous lower lip. "There's no time to do everything I've wanted. We'd be here for days. No, I'm not finished with you." He took my bottom lip between his thumb and forefinger, pulling on it. "You have so much anger."

Why was he bringing that up now? I wanted to lose myself in him, get drunk off Calyse more than I already was, not be reminded of all the turmoil I felt inside. I tried to escape from his hold.

"I want you to let it out. Everything. All that human fury. Try to tear me apart. And while you do, I'm going to fuck you." He had brought his gorgeous face close to mine, a challenge in his expression like I saw in the training area. "All right?"

Need pulsed against my every nerve. "Yes."

He stretched to untie me—a spectacle of muscle—and I was free.

It was a flurry of fingernails scraping and hands grasping and his body weight held me down as I struggled, and he was inside me and I cried out my rage and ecstasy. We were a chorus of effort, grunts and groans as we ground hard against each other. I scratched his back and bit hard into the meat of his shoulder, holding on as I threatened to fling apart. My hands felt down to his straining ass, flexing as he pounded inside me. I dug my nails in.

He roared, driving into me with more abandon. I could barely breathe he was so heavy on top of me. I let out a cry, letting the wild, aching sensation take me. He covered me completely, safe and dangerous all at once. I relished his sweat-covered body pressing against my own.

He was growling. He was animal. He pushed himself inside so far I thought he had grown. With the jerky movements of someone falling, he grabbed first me—my neck, my chest—and then the blankets to the side of us. He was close.

"Come inside me," I ordered, on the edge of release myself.

His neck strained and head fell back as a fragmented shout erupted from him. His hot cum shot inside me, breaking the last of my hold. I gripped the parts of him I could reach as my plea-sure spiked high and piercing. My back arched up from the bed, damp hair spreading around my head thrown back.

Reality returned slowly.

Calyse's thick arm around my waist as he fell on his stomach beside me.

Playfulness returning to his look, replacing the feral beast from a moment before.

His lips taking mine in a tender kiss as he fought to catch his breath.

"You are... my every fantasy," he said.

I could have said the same.

## 20

I didn't want to take my eyes off Calyse, the sheer beauty of him, but now that the haze of our declarations—both verbal and physical—was starting to dissipate and we could think beyond our most primal urges, we had to consider what had happened in the Den.

Calyse had killed the bird woman. His bloody knife still leaned against the wall. But was that enough to stop Im Scathail from attacking or possessing my sister?

I'd been so broken after the encounter that Calyse had halted his mission to tend to me.

And I loved him for it.

Now, we were allies. We both felt it as we sat up and our minds began to clear. Neither of us wanted to put clothes back on and, besides, my dress had ripped fully down the middle.

"I need to check the Den," Calyse said regretfully, running the back of his fingers down my arm.

"I know."

"There weren't many shadows in that woman, so..." The weight of all his fears settled heavy on his massive shoulders.

I touched them gingerly, remembering how my nails had dug so fiercely into his skin. His back would be bloody.

He watched me, amusement finding its way back to his features. "Worried about me?"

"Will you be all right?"

"After fucking you, absolutely. With the Shadow... I won't know until I hear from the others at the party and patrol to make sure."

My hand traced the landscape of his back. No blood. My brows lowered. "But..."

He laughed. "We don't look like this for hundreds of years by chance. I wouldn't be nothing but scars by now if my wounds didn't heal quickly."

"But I've seen burnt and disfigured Fae." I realized that I'd seen more forest creatures with disfiguring marks, but the point still stood.

"We're difficult to kill," he said, standing. The mattress bucked up without his weight. "But not impossible."

"The Enemy?"

"Or each other." A wicked little smirk twisted his lips. He brought his face close to mine. "But your fingernails? No."

I had to battle down my rising lust and focus on the future. "You don't think the shadows were all destroyed?"

"Let's see." He donned new leather armor and cleaned the blood off his knife. His gaze slid back to me. "Maybe you shouldn't accompany me."

I scoffed, striding to the wardrobe. All his clothes would look huge on my thin frame, but I selected a particularly long shirt and belted it together with rope hanging on one side of the apothecary cabinet.

Calyse's eyes blazed as he watched me. "You're trouble," he mused. "All right. Let's discover if the threat still stands." The twinkle in his eye turned distant and solemn, layered with years of disappointed hopes.

How had he managed to find such a playful outlook on life when so much of it had been spent in violent misery? My heart twisted for him.

Together, we mounted the steps to the level above. My suggestive ensemble didn't create an uproar as it would have in Selene, but a few other Fae noticed me—noticed *us*—with a spark of understanding and interest. Personally, I was proud to be seen with him.

We had hardly reached the entrance to the Den when another fiery-haired Fae approached Calyse.

"There were two more inside," he reported, his eyes skimming me for a split second.

"You dealt with them?" Calyse asked.

"Yes. We're disposing of the bodies now."

"Anyone we know?"

The Fae gave two names I'd never heard. Judging from Calyse's even reaction, I suspected they didn't mean much to him either. Endymion and Laura hadn't been possessed by the darkness, at least.

"Interrogations?" he pressed on.

"We're talking to a few who saw them come in. No indication of origin yet."

"And no unessential information?"

That was obviously code for the great secret they kept. This red-haired soldier must be one of the few who helped Calyse when Endymion was possessed.

"Of course not."

"Very good."

Watching Calyse in his element as a warrior, and not just any warrior but the Fae King's right-hand man, made my body glow.

"We're going to do one more sweep, and then I'll join you."

I raised a brow at Calyse. How much of this investigation could I participate in? I wanted to ask questions, observe offenders, track down the movements of the naked bird woman, but his soldierly confidence reminded me forcefully that I was ill-trained for such things. I'd hate to get in his way. Perhaps I could assist in a separate manner.

"Come on," he said, taking my hand, claiming me.

We'd never held hands. We'd done all that lovers do but that. This gesture was public, possessive.

I loved it.

We walked into the Den. Much of the festive atmosphere had dimmed, leaving only those most abandoned to their vices or sensation. That the party continued at all highlighted how different the Other Kingdom was from the human one. Multiple beings had been killed here. Were those possessed by the Shadow considered so much lesser?

A group of forest creatures clustered along one wall as before. Fae women reclined on the upper platforms.

Sharp copper cut through the fruity scent of wine. The darkness didn't allow me to see anyone's eyes very clearly.

Calyse, without any embarrassment, eased apart couples and interrupted conversations to stare into the guests' faces. No more black.

Perhaps that was it. His problem was over. I gave his big hand an encouraging squeeze.

"Still all right?" he asked me over his shoulder, quiet and deep.

He'd misunderstood the gesture. My mind did incline toward fairy fruit again, but I held Calyse's hand like a talisman. "Yes," I whispered back. "There's no one here."

"No one we're looking for," he agreed. He let out a growling breath.

I couldn't tell if he was upset or aroused. His eyes had gone darker, though not black. It could be both. I saw concern in his features, in the way his eyes still darted warily into the corners, but the place our bodies touched buzzed with mutual awareness.

Pulsing music circled the room like a warm, sucking whirlpool. Every sound, every conversation, sounded furtive. If I didn't have Calyse, the atmosphere would have drowned me again. Now, I was drowning in him, filled with the recent memory of feeling him deep inside me.

With effort, I exhaled slowly and said, "Should we go back to the interr—"

But he was on me, pulling me to him, his lips against mine. My eyes flew wide before I closed them and sank into the kiss. This kiss felt possessive, protective. Before all these people, he marked me as his.

I surrendered to our wild connection. In this place, it would hardly be a matter of comment.

His lips traveled to my ear. "Remember what I said?" he huffed.

"You've said many ridiculous things."

I felt his face stretch into a grin at my neck. Without elaborating, he pushed me up against a clear stretch of wall barely curving away from the main room. Holding me in place with his body, he lavished attention on my lips, my waist, my breasts. When he cupped my breasts, teasing the nipples through the shirt, I gasped. We were in public. Anyone could see us. Just from my line of sight, multiple Fae and forest creatures passed.

"I want to take you here," he said in a voice like gravel.

I panted out a few breaths, considering. He would stop if I asked him to, but, just like every other time, I didn't want him to. I wanted to do terribly bad things with this silly, selfless, powerful, violent Fae.

My heart beat so hard he must have felt it through his shirt. When he pressed more fully against me, I felt his renewed erection bulging between my legs.

"Do it," I breathed.

With quick, expert movements, he lifted up my makeshift dress and undid the clasps on his trousers, freeing his hard length. I wrapped my leg around his hip to make his entrance easier. With a sigh from both of us, he plunged in. The prospect of being watched made me even wetter.

At first, he just kissed me again. Casual guests might think we were passionately snogging in this corner, and that was all.

That was not all. He pushed farther inside me, urging my inner muscles to open for him. I broke the kiss to open my mouth in a silent scream. He used my weakening legs to gain leverage to fill me completely. An unseemly noise escaped me.

Calyse smiled. "You told me to be quiet," he said, breathless.

"You... ah... didn't tell me anything."

What followed could not be mistaken as kissing.

TOO SATISFIED TO CARE ABOUT THE POSSIBILITY OF LINGERING shadows, I stayed that night in the new area set aside for the women of Selene. After Eve's horrible death, none of us wanted to return to the East Wing, so separate accommodations had been arranged about a five-minute walk from it.

Calyse murmured that he wanted me to stay with the others so we could find safety in numbers while he continued his investigation into the Enemy's movements. I would rather have stayed in his bed, but I understood why he didn't want to leave me entirely alone, even in his vault-like room underground. He escorted me, kissed me on the forehead, and promised to return.

It didn't even bother me that the beds here were arranged almost as they had been while we were asleep (and some of us were dead). Each room held eight beds in two neat rows. Sleepily, I looked into the faces of the women before snuggling beneath the covers. No all-black eyes.

I fell almost instantly into slumber.

THOUGHTS OF CALYSE AND THE SHADOW WOKE ME EARLY. I wasn't surprised that the other women hadn't risen yet. All their forms breathed lightly under blankets. I felt the oddest tilt of vertigo, as though I had just awoken in the underground room, parched and disoriented and yearning.

I didn't remember much from that day, but flashes of it returned to me.

"Live long and sleep short," Calyse said. These women lived long but slept long also. They felt, as I had, that there was little else to do.

I sighed, picking out Georgina among them. Quietly, I rose and padded out of the room.

It was odd not to see Calyse at his post, waiting for me. The tiniest stab of apprehension gripped me. Ensuring the castle was free of the destructive shadows must have taken all night. After all, the place was enormous. He would certainly keep Endymion appraised of what was going on as well.

I shook off the sensation and found a table situated in approximately the same configuration as the previous dining table had been.

Dark red spread over this one too.

I sucked in a breath. It wasn't...? No, not blood. I let out a shaky breath. In all the excitement, I hadn't allowed myself to think about Eve's body since that night.

Eve, and then the bird woman.

I swallowed. The red wasn't of blood but of pomegranate seeds. They sprawled across the table in a heap. With my soft movement, a few of them skittered and rolled to the edge of the table. I caught them before they fell. One I squeezed too hard and the juice dripped onto my hand. The liquid fizzed gently against my palm, soaking into the skin. Mesmerized, I burst another seed to watch if it would happen again. Like water on a hot skillet, the pomegranate juice bubbled and became absorbed, lightly tickling.

The fruit's sharp scent filled the air. How had I not noticed it immediately? And the skin glistened like the blood I mistook it for.

Heartbeats galloped in my chest.

This was fairy fruit.

$\maltese$ 21 $\maltese$

The difference between ordinary fruit and the kind I craved was slight externally, but unmistakable. Fairy fruit glittered when it struck the eye. It seduced with smell and taste and texture. It promised fantasy.

I dropped the remaining pomegranate seeds in my hand. Already, my skin had absorbed some of the juice. I could tell. I felt light-headed with drink.

*Turn around.*

But my feet wouldn't obey. I stood rooted, staring. I wouldn't win this battle. No matter how long I held my breath or promised myself that I had no need of fairy fruit, it wouldn't change the longing knocking at my stomach, at my fingers, at my brain saying *eat, eat, eat!*

I groaned with mad frustration at myself and wild joy at my luck. And I ate.

The firm skin of the pomegranate seeds burst like stars on my tongue, releasing the tart, sweet juice. I shoved handfuls into my mouth. There was so much. Maybe I could take some back to my room... No, there were others sharing my room now. There was nowhere to hide it. I had to eat my fill now and hope no one else woke up.

Drops trickled down my chin and onto Calyse's shirt I still wore as a dress. I wanted to bury myself in this heap of fruit, to bathe naked in it, to never stop crunching and sucking and eating fairy fruit.

The fizzing I'd witnessed on my hand continued on my tongue, a strange feeling but not unwelcome. I breathed around huge bites of fruit.

Blinking, I realized I hadn't passed out. Could I... was I stronger now? Could I handle more fairy fruit at once?

Galvanized by the thought, I set to eating with more vigor. Instead of feeling weaker, as though I fought time itself to get my fill, I grew stronger. My very skin felt as though it were stretching from within.

I was cold. I was vicious. I was a being of darkness and teeth.

Something moved in my peripheral vision. A Fae attendant. I scooped up the delicious seeds faster, not wanting to share a single one. The idea coursed despair through me. I couldn't possibly eat them all without someone else emerging and wanting a taste. The Fae weren't gripped by the same desperation as the women of Selene.

My breaths came ragged around my huge bites, my hands and face wet with juice.

The Fae attendant stepped closer. Male. Pale-skinned. Black-eyed.

My grasping hands stilled, just for a moment. No whites shone around the irises. This was supposed to bother me. But he held a basket of fresh pomegranates, not yet shucked.

My cry of delight and need stirred some of the sleeping women, who came out soon after. The attendant patiently stood while I savaged the fruit. Now other hands grabbed for them.

Other mouths ate the seeds. My ecstasy turned into something sharp and painful. I reached out to the others.

But the hands were not my own.

They were made of shadows.

I was two in one, then. Horror and fascination filled me at the sight of fingers of darkness writhing up from my skin and stretching toward the nearest woman. I felt powerful. I was appalling. I couldn't breathe...

"Lizzie!"

An armed, dark-skinned Fae locked eyes with me. He looked so familiar. I was forgetting something I shouldn't.

I'd never seen such a look of utter shock and bereavement. It made me want to cry.

I tried to pull back the shadows in case that was the cause of his horror, but found I couldn't. They coiled around me like snakes, enveloping my body and curling around the women near me. At least they wouldn't take it all if they were smothered by the darkness...

A grunted cry cut through my thoughts as the Fae barreled toward me, sword unsheathed. Would he kill me? I widened my eyes, breath catching.

My shadows darted in his direction. His handsome face, rugged and square, contorted in a snarl as he tried to avoid them. He missed the brunt of them, but the grasping fingers snagged his arm. He hurled himself sideways, out of their grip. Always, his gaze returned to mine. Its intensity pierced me with pain.

I knew him, didn't I?

My brow furrowed as I tried to remember. Those fiery orange eyes, that muscular build...

It was as though a thin sheen of ice had frosted over everything and now cracks had appeared. Through them, I could see flashes of people I knew. I understood, and then I didn't again.

I cried out with frustration. My tongue felt heavy and hot.

The Fae lunged for the black-eyed attendant on his way to me. His swinging sword just missed him. There were too many women crowding around the table, eating the succulent fairy fruit.

I didn't hold any more in my hand. My fingers burned. My tongue burned. My veins burned. My next cry was of pain. The frost of confusion melted faster and faster.

The fairy fruit. There was something wrong with it.

"Stop!" I said, knocking seeds to the ground. Automatically, compulsively, I popped a few into my mouth.

But the women didn't listen. They grew angry, pushing me and my shadows away from the table.

The darkness lashed out, streaming from me now. I felt caught in a cold, rushing river. All I could do was watch as the shadow targeted the woman who had pushed me and forced itself down her throat, a choking torrent. Her skin grew dark and her eyes wide as it filled her. Then, like fire, the shadows broke through the skin, eating it away to shriveling burns.

I tried to step away. Revulsion and horror made my whole body shake, but I couldn't stop what was happening. The burning darkness kept roaring out of me and into her. Desperately, I twisted to the side to break the connection.

Something grabbed me. Was it the shadow, doing to me what it had done to her?

Dead, the woman dropped to the ground.

The evil fruit scorched my insides too. My stomach and skin and everywhere spiked with pain.

Once the woman was dead, the stream of darkness subsided to an ominous cloud of smoke around me. Only I knew that it was eating me next, that I hadn't called upon some dark force to kill that woman on my behalf.

"Help!" I cried feebly. My mouth was so dry I could hardly speak. I tried again. "Help!"

I couldn't move. Arms locked me in place.

I struggled against my captor. I was a victim, not a murderer. Panic sent my heart beating so fast I was afraid it would stall.

"Shhh!" said a voice in my ear. "I have you."

That voice. That big, dark shape.

It was Calyse.

Infinitely relieved and horrified that he was seeing me this way, I turned so I could bury my face against his chest and hold on tight.

He embraced me for only a moment before prying me away from him. He looked into my eyes, anguish pulling at the corners of his mouth. His eyes looked deeper set. Finally, after hesitating, he took me firmly by the upper arms and dragged me away to my room. He threw me in and locked the door.

## 🦋 22 🦋

Alone in my dark room, burning from the inside, smoking with shadows, I slumped to the floor.

Darkness had eaten that woman alive.

Even now, the events of a moment ago felt almost like dreams. My stomach growled in protest at how much fairy fruit I'd devoured at once. As images pieced themselves together, I knew the woman hadn't been Georgina or any of the others I regularly talked to. It didn't matter. She had been alive and now she was dead and it was my fault.

I shrieked and clawed at my skin where the shadows seemed thickest. How could this have happened?

Calyse had said there was a threat in the castle, and I was trying to overcome my addiction to fairy fruit. Yet at the first opportunity, I ate as much as I could, letting in the Enemy.

That's what this was. The Shadow Calyse feared so much now resided in me. Sickness surged up in me at the thought.

Would he have to kill me, as he'd killed the bird woman?

Terror left me shaking. I didn't want to be alone, but I could hurt anyone who came to help me, even Calyse. His expression revealed how torn he felt over the decision to spare me. My throat closed with shame.

At least the burning had subsided to a dull hum beneath my skin. It still felt uncomfortably hot, but I no longer felt like I was dying.

Did it even matter? Would I ever get to see Calyse or Laura or Mother face to face again? Would the latent power in me burst out again and harm someone else?

And, damn my life, I still longed for fairy fruit, even though I already felt sick from eating so much of it. The juice lingered on my chin. I licked it off, a rabid dog licking an oozing sore.

Angry tears welled in my eyes. Before, I was just a burden, a collection of desperate longings, but now I was a violent sickness to be eliminated. I hugged my knees.

The image of Calyse's face returned to my mind. I'd broken his heart. Even as I sat there with my life unraveling, I wished he sat here with me, joking so I'd feel better or holding me so I didn't fall apart. I wanted to apologize. But what could I say? How could I explain what I'd done to wrench apart all the careful work he'd done to rid the palace of Im Scathail over the past century?

It would have been better if we had never met.

Yes, I would have languished without purpose. My recovery—recovery, ha!—would have been so much slower, and my heart would have ached all the more with loneliness. My life would be so much emptier without him. But that still would have been better than this.

Calyse deserved peace, happiness, and I brought him nothing but pain.

I swallowed. If only I could take back my confession from the other night. I did love him. I did want him to be with me in every way. Just the memory of his strong arms wrapped around me stirred the embers of my heart. But he deserved better.

By the time someone opened the door, I was numb and empty.

My life had not ended with the enchanted sleep. Waking then provided a new opportunity.

The end of my life was here, now.

❧

"Don't—" The urgent word halted when my door opened. Pale light sliced through the darkness. I didn't move from my position on the floor.

Calyse rushed inside, head swiveling. He discovered where I was and stood protectively over me, hand on the bloody knife at his belt. I had made myself so small that I only saw the back of his strong legs, braced to defend. Behind him came two others: Laura and Endymion.

I hung my head.

"Lizzie, what happened?" Laura asked, voice breaking. Once Calyse took up his position, she didn't come closer, but stayed at Endymion's side. I knew her body language. She cared about me, but she was afraid. Of me.

All three of them looked disheveled and haggard. Endymion's expression was haughty, chin lifted, lip curled as he gazed down—far down—at me.

If only I could disappear...

"It doesn't matter what happened," said the King in his deep, cultured voice.

"End...." Calyse rumbled the warning.

"She has the Shadow." A fleeting glimpse of regret passed over his features as his golden eyes flicked to the knife. "You know your job."

"To take care of her, you said." I'd never heard Calyse use this tone before. Hard, defiant.

Endymion took one step forward. Calyse's hand tightened on the hilt. The King didn't appear alarmed, even though Calyse looked ready to spring. He kept his insolent calm.

"It must be done."

"End." This time it was Laura. "There has to be another way. We found another way. Please don't."

I could no longer see the writhing shadows pouring off me, but their cold touch caressed me, just underneath the skin of my arm. I jerked back. *Not now. Not now, not now!*

Calyse noticed immediately, despite his heavy focus on the King. He jutted his jaw, not needing to ask what was happening to me. His profile revealed all his lightheartedness gone. Here, he would fight for me, die for me, despairing as a character in one of Laura's stories. It took all my strength to meet his eyes.

The King seemed to understand too. He slid a comforting hand around Laura's waist. "She's a danger."

"Not to me!" Laura snapped, twisting out of his hold. She crouched to peer at me around Calyse's legs. "We'll find a way to free you." Tears glistened in her golden eyes.

I pursed my lips.

"There is no way," the King said, deep and resonant as a funeral bell.

My stomach balled into a knot, not for myself, but for the pain this caused Calyse and Laura. I never meant to hurt them.

"There's no need," I told her. My voice came out brittle and rasping. Then, to Calyse, "I'm sorry. It's all right."

The knot in my stomach had become a knot in my throat and I couldn't get out any more words.

"It's not," he replied, voice low and dangerous. "You have nothing to be ashamed of."

"Calyse," came Endymion's warning.

"I won't harm her."

"Cal—"

"I'd let the world burn first!"

I was totally unprepared for the wildness in his cry. It was intensity. It was resolve.

"Calyse!" I pleaded. His declaration struck something deep in my soul, a parched place that pomegranate juice hadn't filled. I wanted to lean into his protection, to hide myself in him, but I couldn't. "It's not worth it."

"You are." He turned to meet my eyes. "You are." His brow furrowed, determination written in every anguished line.

I was breaking all over again. "How do you know?" I whispered.

Hopefully, he could hear me. His enhanced Fae senses, so attuned to me, would catch my question.

He didn't look away from me as Laura said, "Let me try something."

"Laura," said the King, "I know you care about your sister, but she's lost."

I didn't look away from Calyse, whose kind face and dirty banter and selfless power had drawn me up out of a deep pit of despair. I felt as though I peered up at him from within a well, this time too far to reach. But his face gave me whatever comfort I could still find. I missed him. I missed them all.

I missed myself.

"She can't be lost," Laura insisted. From the corner of my eye, I saw her hands open in the stance she held in the training area. Would she blast me with shadows? Fine.

"Don't hurt her," said Calyse, finally breaking off our long look.

"I'll try not to," she promised.

Endymion swept a long, pale finger over Laura's gold-tipped ear and spoke into it. "What if there's a counter-attack?"

"Then kill me," I said.

"No!" Calyse yanked me to my feet and hid me fully behind his body.

"Move," Laura said gently. "Please. I love Lizzie."

I saw his back rise and fall heavily with panted breaths. Then he moved to stand beside me, resolutely taking my hand in his. He threaded his big fingers through mine and lifted his chin. Whatever they did to me, they would have to do to him.

I wanted to tell him to back away, but I was too weak. I needed his strength. Simply another reason I couldn't stay like this.

I didn't know what I could do to solve this problem, but I knew I had to do something, even if it meant death.

Laura's expression was apologetic but determined. She spread her feet a little wider, drew in a breath, and released a thick rope of darkness.

Calyse's hand tensed in mine. He felt as dangerous as a wild animal. I gripped him more firmly, anchoring him too.

The shadow wound toward me quickly but deliberately, nothing like my out-of-control incineration of the Selene woman. Laura controlled her darkness. It reached my face. Answering cold bubbled up within me. The stream split into sections, entering into my ears, my nose, my mouth.

Endymion glanced searchingly at Laura. Did she know what she was doing?

I surrendered to it. Laura would never willingly hurt me. If she thought that sending in her shadows might help, then I had to believe her. Even if they did harm me, I wouldn't blame her. As an end, for me, it wouldn't be so bad. I got to see her again, and Calyse held my hand.

Like a bottle filling with cold liquid, I froze as more and more darkness searched inside me. I could tell she was searching, though I couldn't pinpoint the sensation that gave that away. The cold burned, setting my teeth on edge. I shut my eyes, leaning into Calyse's strong arm. He was warm and never buckled under my weight.

Something within me snagged, as if an organ low in my gut had been yanked upward. I cried out. Calyse's muscles hardened beneath my cheek.

A brief hesitation, then renewed pulling.

This wasn't right. Laura hadn't found the Enemy—she'd found my intestines or something else necessary. If she kept tugging, I'd be pulled inside out.

"No, wait," I gasped before I could stop myself.

"Wait," Calyse echoed in his general's voice.

"I've found it," Laura said, focused and sure.

Cold battled with heat. I was melting. I would burst into a pile of entrails.

"You're hurting her."

If I opened my mouth, I would scream. But that wasn't what happened.

"King Endymion." The low voice sounded like smoke and wind, ancient and young.

And it came out of my mouth.

## ❧ 23 ❧

Beside me, Calyse recoiled before wrapping his hand around my bicep as though I'd float away. Laura stared at me in disbelief. A vertical line formed between Endymion's brows—long-held hatred.

I couldn't speak. I felt as insubstantial as a child's toy, picked up and used in any way the owner chose.

"And Queen Laura," Im Scathail said in a sneer.

She lowered her hands, the shadows snuffing out.

"You are a plague to me. It is my nature to expand and fill and know all life." The voice emanating from me was more ancient than the Fae, perhaps wiser. I couldn't keep my own thoughts in line. "Your petty attempts to destroy me have ended in failure, accomplishing nothing but to stoke my anger."

"Leave her alone!" Laura cried, eyes streaming. I admired the ferocity in her face. Or was that *his* admiration?

"That's enough," muttered Endymion, afraid for the first time.

Pressure on my arm said Calyse hadn't moved. Metal rang as he unsheathed his knife. The King and his best friend glared at each other.

"Perhaps now, this"—I, he, looked around imperiously—"will finally let you rest from your fight. You want to rest. You know it will come when I have victory here. There will be no more resistance, only peace."

Calyse swallowed loudly. Darkness rose from my body in great smoky swaths. I could have risen from the floor and now been surprised, so thoroughly was I not in control of myself. My thrashing heart was the only indication I still existed within the cage of myself.

"Thank you for keeping those maidens for me," Im Scathail continued, almost wistful. "Their minds are ripe for me with only the slightest urging." He moved my free hand down the front of my body. "This one appears to matter to you."

Laura twitched.

"Lizzie," Calyse said into my ear. "Lizzie, I'm here with you." It was the tone of a person who knows they will die soon. A last stand.

The Enemy wouldn't let me answer. His next words were slow and menacing, grating like the rocks in the making of the world. "Let me."

Heaving in a breath, Endymion charged forward, a blade appearing in his hand.

Lightning quick, Calyse met his knife. Their joined blades weren't so much as a hand's span away from my stomach. Watching felt as detached as if this were a play. Both Fae men bared their teeth, bestial and fierce. Neither wanted to hurt the other, but the alternative was too terrible for either to contemplate.

I, in the center of this conflict, had no freedom at all.

Choking on sobs, Laura shot shadows from her hands again. They entered, icy, down my throat, into my head, down my torso, into my breasts, my arms, my stomach, my core. The shock made me convulse. This time, she wasn't careful. She found the same spot as before, that essential piece, and gripped tightly.

My vision blurred. The room had been dark before with only the light from the doorway slicing through. Now black fog rolled through it until I could see nothing at all.

From within Im Scathail's frustration, I felt my own panic, clear and sharp. What was happening to the others? Was I hurting them?

I floated in a roiling sea, skin chilled by the waves. All was utterly dark.

I opened my mouth. No sound came out.

I tried again. I was still here, deep inside, though held down by this ancient force. Laura's shadows ripped at me.

With all the energy I had, I called out their names. The sound was a whisper, tiny, but it passed the barrier to land on the air. "Cal. Laura."

I heard Laura scream with effort and rage, and then I was screaming as my body tore like Eve's on the table. Inside to outside. Laura's shadows yanked my soul out of my mouth. In a crash of ice and fire, I crumpled to the ground.

⁂

IN THE DARKNESS, I BURNED. VOICES SPOKE ABOVE ME, churning like a whirlwind. A thumb smoothed my lips, my eyelids.

I wrenched open my eyes.

Someone gasped. My entire body hurt as though I'd been pulled out of shape and squashed back haphazardly into the form of a girl.

Lips found mine, desperate and relieved. Calyse. I loved him so much I couldn't contain it in my small frame. I felt I would burst apart. The sweetness of his lips was like the sweetness of fairy fruit. I couldn't get enough because I knew it would be gone soon. All that beautiful sensation would leave me empty, but I had him for now.

He broke the kiss first. His orange eyes had gone red around the edges. Laura knelt beside me as well, her skin gray.

"Your... your eyes!" she exclaimed.

"What?" Were they still black? Was Im Scathail still lying latent inside me? I curled up tighter in Calyse's lap.

"They're blue."

My mouth fell open. "Blue?" They hadn't been blue since before I entered the forest. Did that mean...?

"Not Fae blue," she explained. "Blue like they were before."

Calyse dipped back into my line of sight. "They are," he breathed.

Laura, Calyse, and even Endymion, standing a little distance away, all had fiery golden eyes. They hadn't changed. So what had happened to me?

"Check the others!" Endymion ordered to someone just outside the door. He approached me to get a closer look. Laura stood and he slid a hand around her waist. The King exchanged a fraught glance with Calyse.

The two of them had fought over me—Endymion to kill and Calyse to defend. I couldn't blame either one. But Calyse's insubordination could earn him a strong punishment. I didn't know all the laws of the Fae, but I knew that sudden, violent retribution was often the way.

I struggled to sit higher. My stomach kneaded with nausea, but now my body covered more of his. If Endymion struck out with a knife, he'd have to kill me too. Perhaps he would. He hadn't hesitated before.

Calyse's hands propped me higher on his lap before anchoring me in place, demonstrating his choice and defenselessness.

"If her eyes are blue," Laura said, snatching the King's attention, "does that mean she could return to Selene?"

I heard the longing in her voice. Returning was something she could never do.

My heart thumped at the idea. I'd given up my old life because I had to. Now, I had a new decision to make. Before the thought finished flowing through my mind, I'd made my choice.

"I think it does," Endymion conceded, kissing her temple absently.

"Because the curse is broken?" Laura's question was a broken, hopeful whisper.

The King's eyes blazed as if he stood on a precipice, overlooking a newly won kingdom, but he didn't answer.

Around me, Calyse's arms gave the slightest tremble. If Im Scathail was gone, if the curse was broken, then his years of danger and suffering were over. I squeezed his hand.

I could leave him in peace, then.

We were nothing but a chorus of hard-beating hearts until the Fae Endymion had commanded returned.

"Their eyes no longer match ours, and the fruit has been disposed of."

Something twisted hard behind my sternum at both pieces of news.

Laura let out a sob and fell against her husband's side.

Endymion extended a hand toward Calyse, who grasped it in a soldier's grip of solidarity.

"Had you not served me so long..."

"I know, End. I was prepared to face the consequences."

This bittersweet triumph flowed around me without penetrating my heart. I wanted to rejoice as well. I was free from the curse that didn't allow me to return to my village. Laura's effort had defeated the great enemy of the Fae. It was glorious.

But my weakness had let him in, threatening them all. Perhaps the Shadow wouldn't have earned a strong foothold if I'd been stronger.

I gave Laura a wan smile. "Thank you," I said, leaning back more firmly into Calyse's broad chest.

"I would do anything for you," she replied.

I knew it was true. Through her efforts, the women had woken from their sleep. Because of her, the dark force no longer possessed me. But what could I do for her?

"I'll take Lizzie to rest," Calyse announced, lifting me in his arms. How had he known I couldn't walk? "You tell the maidens there's nothing more to fear."

Above me, his cheek crinkled in a smile, but it was a tired version of the usually jovial expression he wore.

"I can rest here," I said. I was in my room, after all.

"You shouldn't be alone right now," he murmured. My bed was only large enough for one.

I closed my mouth and allowed him to carry me out of the room. His body rocked around me as he walked, lulling me into a trance-like state of exhaustion. I couldn't celebrate. I could barely be happy that Laura and Calyse were willing to sacrifice themselves for me. I loved them, so why would they jeopardize themselves for someone so unworthy of their affection?

He took me down great hallways and open rooms, colonnades and antechambers, down the flight of stairs to the private lower level. Finally, we reached his room and he set me gently on the bed.

Only days ago, I'd been so happy and in love. I thought I was getting better. My love for Calyse hadn't waned, but my belief in myself had evaporated.

I curled on my side, away from him. Hot shame flooded my face.

"Lizzie, my love," he said, touching my shoulder.

"Nemesis," I corrected, half a sob.

The mattress lowered as he tucked in next to me, around me. His gestures were so tender, so sure and strong, that I broke. My back hitched as I started to cry.

"I'm sorry," I managed.

He traced a finger down the side of my face. "It's not your fault."

"It is!" Anger welled up. "I let him in."

"The Enemy is a wicked ancient spirit—*was* a wicked ancient spirit. He used you."

"Because he could."

Calyse rolled me toward him. I didn't want to look in his face and lose my resolve. I knew what I had to do, and I didn't want to do it. Compassion shone in his fiery eyes. His thick strands of black hair fell crazily on the pillow. The full lips parted slightly. Memories of kissing those lips so hard they bruised rose to mind. The times I'd given myself fully to him, to *us*, so sweet at first and then feral in our need.

I tried to steel my broken heart, but found it too difficult while I was looking back in his rugged, handsome face.

"Everything I said about you is true," he said in an undertone. "This doesn't make me love you any less. You survived something that no one else has before." The ghost of a smile bloomed on his face. "You surprise me and... I'm more convinced now of your strength than I was before. I'm fucking obsessed." He cupped his hand soothingly on my shoulder. "You don't have to say anything or do anything now. Just rest. You've had a terrible day. But your strength has helped free us all."

I scoffed.

He caught the noise with his mouth on mine. "You have."

No matter how much I protested, he wouldn't believe me. I flexed my foot, testing if I had enough strength to move it, to stand.

To walk out of here as soon as he fell asleep.

❧ 24 ❧

Calyse often said, "May you live long and sleep short." I didn't realize that meant he wouldn't sleep all night. In my exhaustion, I dozed, but Calyse held me firmly against him the whole time.

Why was he making this so difficult for me? I was trying to do the right thing, the hard thing, but all I wanted in the deep hours besides rest was his body carefully lavishing itself on mine. I needed to memorize the scent of him, the way his hands felt at my waist or his teeth felt grazing my ear.

"Can you... Can Fae sense thoughts?" I murmured, barely articulate, into his neck. I was almost too warm, pressed against him like this, but it felt good.

"What do you need, my love?"

"An'ser."

Above my head, his muscles moved just a little. A smile. If only I could crawl inside him and stop being myself...

"They can't read thoughts. You have to tell me."

A tiny part of me had feared that they could, since I didn't know the full extent of their abilities. At least Calyse wouldn't know my plans to leave him. He would try to convince me to stay, and I'd shown in plenty of ways that I wasn't strong enough to withstand such intense temptation.

I only hum-groaned in answer, taking a deep breath and nestling closer.

He tightened his arms around me. I pushed back so I could peel off my dress and reconnect skin to skin. Lying sideways, creaky and sleepy and sore, made the movement awkward. He helped me throw it to the side of the bed.

The sun must have been less than an hour away. I needed to run, but if Calyse was never going to fall asleep...

No wonder I had thought Fae could understand thoughts. Calyse tenderly kissed my breasts, still soft and warm with sleep. I inhaled a deeper breath than I'd taken in hours. His mouth wasn't hurried, but slow, savoring. He licked and sucked my nipples with none of the violence that had characterized our earlier sex. With each sweep of his tongue, each gentle brush of his hand, I felt his love. I'd been fancied, liked, lusted after, but never adored like this.

He hummed his pleasure into me. When we connected like this, I never felt ashamed. I was Lizzie and he was Calyse. Enough.

At least, enough for now.

I banished the thought to the morning and reached down between his legs. Finding his cock, already half-hard, I eased it above the waistband and gently, just as gently as he was touching me, massaged him. I made little circles on the head with my thumb, teased the skin, languorously pushed and pulled, up and down.

There was no hurry and no hesitation. Our breathing became deep and luxurious as we savored each other. I tried to tell him everything in those strokes, those kisses.

*I love you.*

*I'll miss you so terribly I'm not sure I'm strong enough to bear it.*

*I'd rather be with you than anywhere else.*

Calyse's strong fingers moved down—purposefully but carefully—to my center. They slid between the folds. He swiped up and down along my crease, building up an ache of pleasure wherever he pressed.

I knew he wasn't only moving slowly because of how physically fragile I felt after the possession. He wanted to give me time to tell him to stop if I wasn't emotionally ready. Though I didn't feel emotionally ready for much, Calyse's gentle lips and fingers would always be welcome. He made me feel safe, even in the way he ravished me. We'd stood in the middle of a party and he'd fucked me up against a wall and I'd still felt safe.

This was different, a bald confession. Maybe my heart would finally break.

I channeled my thoughts into my pumping hand, increasing the speed and pressure. He mimicked the movement along my clit. Even his tongue, still on my breast, matched the speed. We synchronized perfectly.

My breath escaped in little gusts. I pressed harder, and he pressed harder, slipping a finger inside. Tiny movements of his hips proved he was thrusting into my hand. His dick had become heavy and hard.

I wanted all of him inside all of me. Soon enough, I wouldn't have his warmth, and he could mend and find someone better, someone who wouldn't hurt him. For now, I was selfish. Add that to my many vices.

I moaned and threw one leg over his so he could slide in deeper. Still gentle, he thrust his fingers through my slippery skin, pumping and exploring for those places that would make me writhe, desperate for more. Everywhere, he searched for what I needed in that moment. He didn't push me past what I was giving to him.

The ground seemed to crater beneath me, inviting me to fall. I could let Calyse love me, but then what?

No. I'd already caused him pain and I wasn't finished yet. My fractures were too deep. I didn't belong in this world where Im Scathail no longer tormented him. He deserved the chance to be free.

Desperately, I clung to him. Seconds ticked by somewhere, forcing me closer to the moment when I would have to take my opportunity and run.

He was thick and hard in my hand. I squeezed and drew him closer to my entrance.

In the frenzy of the moment, I didn't understand why he stilled. His fingers drew out of me. When he wouldn't press any closer, I finally met his eyes. They were hooded and concerned.

"Lizzie," he said, "maybe not now."

A ball of frustration and sorrow hardened in my stomach. "Why not?" I snapped before instantly regretting my tone.

He kissed my lips, the hint of his tongue tasting them. "Let's just rest," he whispered.

Defiant, I gripped his cock more firmly.

"Lizzie..." His grated word was a warning. He reached down beneath the covers and found my fingers wrapped around him. He forced his fingers between mine. Now we both held him. By the hardening beneath the soft skin, I could tell the sensation jolted him as it did me.

"I want to make you come," I confessed. There was more— much more—behind that confession. Hopefully, he would allow me this one victory.

A dimple formed in his cheek as he hesitated, holding himself rigid. I cupped his cheek with my free hand and kissed that dimple. "Please," I said against his skin.

He blew out an exasperated breath, mouth twisting a little in a smile. "You dirty... little... nemesis." We pulled on his cock between each word. I let him take the lead, paying attention to the nuances of where his hand went, the tempo, the pressure. As much as I could, I tried to copy and enhance his movements.

He entranced me. Watching his expression was a gift. It went focused, then dreamy, then clenched, then ecstatic. Nothing existed for him but us, this.

We sped up. The ridges of our fingers rose above the crown, bringing down some of the wetness. He grew slippery and urgent. His quiet sounds grew guttural.

I struggled to keep pace, held in place by his own strong fingers. He was showing me both how he wanted to be loved and that he would be all right on his own. At least, that was how I tried to see it.

Struck with inspiration, I held my free hand over his mouth. "Not yet," I said. I wanted this to last as long as I could draw it out.

He struggled to speak around my hand. The noises indicated he wouldn't last. His cat-like eyes rolled back.

"Not yet," I demanded.

He growled and focused enough to shoot me a glare.

Then, "I want you to look at me while you do it." I removed my hand from his mouth. He caught the tip of my thumb between his teeth, smiling wickedly.

The smile faded, replaced with the surprise and tension of a coming orgasm. Our hands between us pulsed urgently. His hips trembled. With a tremendous amount of concentration, he glued his attention on me as his mouth ratcheted open, releasing throaty moans as he came.

I peeled my sticky fingers from his cock, unthreading them from his. My body was filthy with him. Already, I missed this intimacy.

My body was filthy.

It was an excuse to freshen up, to stand. Calyse had a pool in his room, as well as a sink, though, so would the ruse work?

I seemed to be made of stone. I couldn't move.

"You insisted," he said in a rasp, blurry and happy as he leaned into my lips. He made a louder growling sound than the rumbles that usually escaped him in bed. "I can't believe I'm yours. Together we'll get you through everything—what just happened, all of it. My love's big enough to eat the world."

My eyes stung as I returned one last kiss before sitting up. The air felt cold away from Calyse's heat.

"I'm a mess," I chastised. "I need to get myself together."

He raised a thick, disheveled eyebrow. "And then rest?"

A miniature cage closed around my heart, squeezing until I thought it would burst. My plan was working.

"And then rest."

A knock at the door cut off my words. Fae rarely knocked, and I already knew that sound. It was Laura.

Calyse was already out of bed, adjusting himself in his trousers. He opened the door. "My Queen," he greeted.

"Is she sleeping?" Laura whispered. I couldn't see her.

I sighed. "No," I groaned.

Laura's blonde head peeked around Calyse. "Lizzie, I wanted to check on you." Her voice sounded weak and watery, as though she too hadn't slept. Im Scathail had stolen some of her strength last night as well. As much as I wanted to run into my sister's arms, the damage I had caused her only fed my resolve.

"I'm taking care of her," Calyse said.

"But is she *sleeping?*" The way she emphasized the last word suggested she knew exactly what was going on between the two of us.

"Yes," he grunted.

Holding a sheet over my bare chest didn't strengthen his argument.

"Would you walk with me?" she asked from the doorway. When I hesitated, she added, "*Can* you walk?"

I nodded, determined to do it. I hadn't tried since the possession. I hoped so. I'd been able to move my legs a few minutes ago, but they hadn't been bearing my weight.

A laugh bubbled in my gut. When had I ever worried about walking or moving or doing any of those things a young woman should be able to do? I felt old.

I slipped my dress back over my head. When I cast a look back, I caught the end of an unapologetic shrug from Calyse. His eyes twinkled, not with conquest but with mischief and love. It was as potent a combination as any fairy fruit. Wrenching my mind back to my plan didn't get easier.

"Come here," she said, drawing me into her arms as I approached.

I hugged her back. In Selene we'd had friends, Mother, Grandmother, even Great-grandmother, but no one could replace what we had with each other. She was my closest confidante and best friend, and I know I was hers.

Before we left, something in my stomach jolted. This might be another way to slip from Calyse's watchful gaze into the woods leading back home. In fact, with only Laura for company, it probably would be. I might never see him again.

Trying not to make the farewell obvious, I touched his arm and gave him a quick kiss as Laura swept me from the room.

❧ 25 ❧

"End has been checking everywhere, and it's true. Im Scathail is gone." Laura peered meaningfully into my now blue eyes.

I took her hand. "Are you all right?" Her white hands showed no sign that she had been the one to reach inside with her shadows and wrestle him out, after all. The entire episode washed me with hot shame.

"Just a little tired," she admitted. "I didn't sleep either."

"I slept."

She eyed me with a look I'd taught her.

"Here and there," I hedged.

My limbs, now that I was upright and walking with her down the marble hallway, dragged, brittle as twigs. I squared my jaw and set one foot forward and then another. I would walk. Not only that, but I would walk out of here and through the forest to Selene.

Syrupy, bone-deep weariness threatened to crush me.

"I've been trying to figure out how he could get to you." I recognized a familiar worry in Laura's voice.

"He can't anymore, you said."

"But what—" She stole a look at me. "What should I have done to protect you?"

My guilt twisted into sharp irritation. "Nothing," I snapped. "That's not your responsibility."

"Of course it is!"

"So you foisted Calyse on me."

"That seemed to work out just fine."

She met my stare. Laura was no longer the frightened, cautious girl I once knew. I wanted to know this new version of Laura better. Too bad there wasn't time.

"Is Endymion angry that Calyse defended me?" I asked.

"If it were anyone else, he would have run him through," she said, more casually than I would have thought possible. "But he loves Calyse."

She paused.

She was giving me an opening to talk about my feelings for him.

I wouldn't take it. "That's good. I was concerned there might be bad blood between them."

"Never." She lowered her voice. "Calyse killed him, remember?" A nervous laugh escaped her at the absurdity of it.

"I'm sorry you had to see him like that." Imagining Calyse dead brought bile to my throat. The nearest brush he'd had with death since I knew him was when the Shadow took me and threatened to pour in a torrent down his throat. I crossed my arms.

"So am I." She heaved a breath. "I was so hopeful too. I thought we'd solved it. Did I tell you we rode back to Selene for that golden brush and paint? They were connected to the Oakmaiden and we didn't know it. It's too bad you never got to see her. Lizzie, the Oakmaiden was like a creature from one of my stories—"

"You snuck back to Selene? Did you see Mother?" It was as though a new light sprang up out of the dark. Laura knew the way out of the castle and through the woods to our house. I'd been so concerned with leaving Calyse that the practical details of such a journey had barely crossed my mind.

"I couldn't talk to anyone," she said, bowing her golden head in regret. Perhaps she didn't want me to see her cry. She'd seen me cry plenty of times since I'd woken in that room, far more than she'd seen in the village. "To think they're only half an hour away. I'd give anything to talk to them now. Anything but you or End, that is."

I tried not to sound too suspicious. "Had you left the palace itself before that?"

She shook her head. Pointing further down the hall, she said, "I stayed in a room down there."

I wondered if it looked like Calyse's room. "Which one?"

Her eyes brightened. "I wonder if it's unlocked. I could show you." Her enthusiasm told me that she was glad to have found a benign topic that interested me. No one knew better than Laura that I hadn't been myself these past few months.

"For the most part, I didn't even leave this floor," she explained as we walked. "I just went to the library or the dining room and back. I didn't know about your door until later, or about the door leading outside." She pointed vaguely to each location as she named it.

We'd passed so close to the outside door that she tapped its sculpted metal handle. Now it faded behind us. Could I remember where it was?

"Hm," I said, heart beating fast.

My twiggy legs struggled to match Laura's increased pace,

even though I was taller. I still hadn't made a mental map of the pathways down here. Hopefully, she would lead me the same way again once I saw the room where she was kept.

Strange that, after staying so long in the same palace, I'd never seen it. The gap between her life and mine echoed behind my ribcage.

*It's better for her, for Calyse, for all of them*, I reminded myself.

The corridor dead-ended. Laura turned, almost shyly. This was the one.

She turned the handle and peeked inside. It looked darkly abandoned. When she opened the door wider, illumination from the hallway spilled in enough to let her see to light a candle.

The bedroom was reminiscent of Calyse's, though a little smaller. It too had an inset pool and a large bed, but no apothecary cabinet, desk, or weapons on the walls. This was a softer, more feminine version.

"You were kept here?" I asked softly. In my turmoil, I hadn't considered Laura's situation enough. She had also been a prisoner, also fallen in love...

"Yes." She turned to me with glistening eyes. "I fought for you the whole time." Her voice almost broke.

I scooped her into my arms.

"I didn't know you were here too. I thought you were lost," she said into my shoulder.

"I shouldn't have run into the forest." I laughed drily. "You were right about my engagement to James. I wouldn't have been happy."

"No, it was the kindest thing you could have done. And that book you gave me for my birthday...!"

"Shhh." As I stroked her back, my eyes brimmed too. Hearing her say those words loosened something tight in me. Someone, at least, would understand my actions after this. Perhaps she could explain them to the others.

We held each other in silence for a while, each remembering our foray over the barrier and our fight with Im Scathail.

I kissed her temple. "You've had a hard day. You need hot cocoa and Endymion, and I need to sleep." I gave her a hug before letting go. "Thank you for showing me this place. I see why you caught his eye."

She shot me a skeptical look.

"Really!" I protested. "An innocent human girl who is not only beautiful, but brilliant and tenacious? I'd fall for you in his place."

At that, she laughed. "You're delirious."

"I bet you told him off, and I bet no one had done that in years. He couldn't help but tingle for you."

"I think you're right about sleep."

"And Endymion."

She quirked her lips to the side, chastising me lightly for the innuendo but not disagreeing. "You and Calyse?" she guessed, deflected.

I swallowed thickly and shrugged. "We get along sometimes. Other times I hate him."

Her gaze was knowing. With a small nod, she said, "He's chosen you. I've never seen him like he was earlier."

*When he threatened his best friend to defend me at my worst...* I dropped my eyes.

"Be careful with him."

It took all my strength not to reveal my grief and guilt. No words seemed a fitting response, so I didn't respond.

Although she fixed me with a curious look, Laura didn't press. My last day had been hellish too. Emotions were a ravening animal, striking wherever it found weakness.

"I'll walk you back." Laura, straight-backed as a queen, threaded back through the twisting corridors to Calyse's room.

There was the way leading outside. The handle was a duo of butterflies cast in metal.

*Butterflies, butterflies...*

"I can find the room now," I said once we had walked a few more steps. "Thank you for coming down." Then, because I couldn't help it, "I love you, Laura."

She smiled, slowing. "I love you, Lizzie." She inspected me briefly. Finding nothing to cause additional alarm, she finally said, "Get some sleep." Her mouth opened with more words, but she didn't say them.

I already knew what they were. *Be careful.* It was such a typical thing for Laura to say, but had she voiced it, the words would have carried more sting. I hadn't been careful and I'd fallen prey not only to fairy fruit but also, through it, the Enemy himself. I was grateful she didn't say it.

"I will."

With a swish of her dress, she left in the opposite direction, disappearing around a corner. I strained to listen for the door I knew she had to open to go upstairs.

There. A soft click.

Alone at last, I held my breath. This was it. I retraced my steps until I reached the butterflies. The handle felt cold against my palm. What if it was locked? With two hands, I heaved my weight backward, yanking the door with me.

It gave.

A cold gust of air carried the sweet smell of hay. Without more thought, I slid through the opening. My first guess had been correct. A stable.

Lanterns glowed on posts to reveal three enormous horses looking curiously at me. I had some experience riding, though these mounts far exceeded any beast I'd ever ridden. They were magnificent. They must have belonged to King Endymion, since Calyse had said that few came down here apart from the two of them. And Laura, when she tried to rescue me.

She had done her best, and I was so thankful, but it was time for me to do something for them.

Ornate saddles did sit at one end of the space, but it would take me a while to get all the tack on. If Calyse woke up and looked for me...

I couldn't risk it. Bareback riding wasn't something I liked, but I could do it.

One less thing missing from the stable.

I located the smallest horse, a black and white mare who still stood taller than any horse in Selene, led her out of the stall, and hoisted myself onto her back. My joints creaked. For a moment, the room spun. Every muscle protested. Even my skin prickled with cold. I hadn't thought about the fact that it was no longer summer, as it had been when I ran into the woods.

The villagers of Selene would shake their heads at me. The knowledge felt familiar and grounding enough for me to cling more firmly to the horse's mane.

Soon enough, I'd be back among them. *At least I get to see my family*. I'd always gotten along with Grandmother in particular. I could still make some kind of life there.

With no fairy fruit.

No Laura.

No Calyse.

Feebly waving off despair, I clucked to the mare and spurred her out of the stable.

❧ 26 ☙

Laura's estimate of half an hour had missed the mark. I headed east on the mare, over lightly snowed ground. The sun had risen, blazing rays in my eyes. It wasn't just my exhausted body insisting that this trip took more than half an hour. The sun declared it with cursed brightness.

A visceral ache pulled me back to the castle, but I pressed on. Since I only wore a thin dress, my skin had gone bloodless with cold.

My focus on the trail slipped sideways into voices and memories.

The wild nights with Calyse. His body filling mine. His wicked smirk, kind for all that, always checking with me or knowing what I needed.

Laura's acceptance of my decision to take care of her and the family by marrying the well-to-do baker.

More than once I almost fell off the broad back of the horse.

Ahead, the trees either looked familiar or I was seeing phantoms. No, the forest thinned somewhat here. My heavy eyes didn't deceive me.

The mare shied gently.

I tried to focus on the ground, on my surroundings. What spooked her? I saw nothing. Maybe I was going crazy or she sensed my tenuous hold on consciousness.

"What?" The word came out a slur. I wavered.

Urging her forward, I spasmed when she jolted backward again. Unreasonably upset, I tried again, but it was as though an invisible barrier—

The barrier.

I'd reached it, and the mare couldn't pass. Although I knew the barrier was invisible, it was strange seeing this proof of it without seeing the barrier itself. I'd wandered past it that night without realizing it.

Shivering and weak, I half-jumped, half-fell off the horse. It was a Fae creature. Surely, it could find its way back to the stable on its own.

I took a stumbling step forward, the thin layer of icy snow freezing my bare feet. The next few moments meant nothing but step, breathe, step, breathe.

Through the trees, I smelled smoke. The scent brought a lump to my throat.

A few steps later, I burst from the tree line into the village of Selene. There, to the right, was my house. I pivoted toward it, got my legs tangled, and fell hard.

The world was real and not real. I thought I'd never see this place again, yet here it was, but I felt as though I were a ghost visiting it, not a real woman.

I breathed, cheek pressed against the frozen ground. Darkness swirled as surely as it had after I'd eaten the pomegranate seeds.

Shouting. Feet on the earth. I felt the vibration of their running steps.

My name.

"Lizzie? Lizzie!"

I couldn't tell who it was, but someone rolled me onto my back.

"She's half-frozen! Bring her inside."

Clumsy arms from two or three people lifted me and bore me along. I wanted to protest the speed because it created a breeze on my face, which already felt piercing and tight with cold.

They set me down. Struggling to look around, I saw the bakery. The air felt warm in here and smelled of yeast. I shook convulsively.

"Get her blankets. And tell the women."

*The women* were my family.

I focused on the faces above me, framed by the pitched wooden roof. The sheriff and another man I didn't know very well —perhaps Mr. Pruett?

My attempts to speak all failed. My lips felt like the wooden pieces of a puppet. I didn't know what I would say anyway.

"Lizzie? Lizzie's back?" This voice I knew. James, the baker, the one I'd become engaged to right before I entered the forest.

His embrace nearly smothered me. He wore an apron and still had bits of dough clinging to the pale hair on his arms. "How...?" he began, voice husky.

"Let her rest. I'm sure we'll hear the whole story," said the sheriff.

A blanket materialized and someone sat me up and placed a hot cup in my hands. The clay burned my palms, but I clung to the mug anyway.

I met the sheriff's eyes. His mother, Georgina, would be so proud of him. "Geo..."

By now a crowd by Selene's standards had started to form around me. The bakery probably had never had so many people inside at once. Everyone gawked and fawned over me as if I were lost treasure.

"Move!"

Mother parted the knot of people. Her red face, more lined even than the last time I'd seen her several months ago, contorted when she saw me. She fell to her knees at my feet, sobbing. Behind her stood Grandmother, scowling at the men crowding me, and Great-grandmother, staring in disbelief.

My breaths came shaky and I leaned forward to grip Mother's arm. "I'm here." My thick voice didn't sound right, but at least I could speak.

As surreal as this moment was, everyone's relief at seeing me suggested I had done the right thing by returning. I hoped so. My chest ached simultaneously for my place in front of the fire in our cottage and for the wild, beautiful Fae world.

"Sip your tea," Mother managed.

I smiled. Typical Mother. When I did as she said, the drink tasted grassy, with none of the vitality of Fae food. Certainly nothing like fairy fruit. I shoved the comparison away the best I could. If it meant Calyse and Laura could live free and happy, then I'd eat nothing but potatoes the rest of my life.

"How did you escape?" James asked, crouching beside me.

His presence bothered me. That room right next to me ought to be for Grandmother and Great-grandmother, but the gawking people all but crowded them out.

"And," Mother gasped, "where's Laura?" Her eyes glittered with fear laced with painful hope.

For some reason, I hadn't anticipated that question. I should have. In fact, I hadn't anticipated that there would even be this many questions. When I considered my return, the image of a quiet life before the fire, like a portrait frozen in time, was all that came to mind.

Foolish.

"She's alive," I said.

Great-grandmother convulsively gripped Mother's shoulder.

"But she can't come here. Did you not get the note she left for you?"

"Note?" The lines in Mother's face deepened.

"She explained what she could in a note just on the other side of the barrier." I almost mentioned the gifts but thought better of it with so many ears around. "You never found it."

"You'll have to show us. Why did she not just come home?"

"She can't. She's..." But how could I explain? "She's... maybe you would call it cursed."

Between the two of us, I was more cursed than she, but I couldn't imply that without breaking Mother's fragile heart.

A warm hand settled on top of mine as I held the mug. James. I pursed my lips.

Focusing on Mother, I said, "Can I... go home?"

Shivers still shook me, adding a layer of pathos to my request. I assume it was that drama that galvanized the crowd to practically lift me and deposit me at the cottage where I'd grown up. Their faces revealed their hunger for answers, but I wasn't ready to tell my story yet. I just wanted to rest.

No, that wasn't right.

I wanted fairy fruit and—even more than that, I realized with a pang—I wanted Calyse.

Even James, officially my fiancé, left me alone at the cottage with the generations of women in my family. Mother ushered me to the best place in front of the little fire. Great-grandmother tucked her yellowing blanket around my legs. Grandmother kept muttering that she couldn't believe it, couldn't believe it, it was a miracle...

"You ought to find the note," I insisted. "Laura left treasures for you."

"Treasures?" Grandmother said sharply, coming out of her repetition.

I attempted a smile. "Yes. The Other Kingdom has so much more than we do. It's beautiful there."

Grandmother scoffed.

"It is."

"She's delirious," said Mother, cutting me off.

"I'm not." Feeling had returned to my feet. I was melancholy, not clueless. "I can tell you where it is."

"Near the barrier." Fear and disbelief edged Mother's tone. Did she not want to believe it?

Of course, the treasures could be gone. After months, it was unlikely that the riches and the note remained if they hadn't already been found. The cracks in my heart widened at the idea that Laura's gift hadn't already brought them joy.

"We don't care about treasures," Mother said more gently. "We care that you're home with us."

At that, tears spilled down her cheeks. Mother was a woman of big emotions, but they usually came out as brusque warnings. Inside, she harbored deep fear and sadness. Because of the tough way she hid them, it had taken me a long time to understand that.

All three generations of women above me surrounded the chair where I sat. Their love reached me like something physical. Their protection and care filled the empty places within me. Just for a moment, but it was a wonderful moment.

"If you don't want to talk about it, that's all—"

"You're so thin!" Grandmother cut in.

I was. I always had been, but the past few months hadn't been kind to me. Only one thing had gotten me through, and he wasn't here.

"Were you with the goblin men?" Great-grandmother warbled. She was stick-thin herself, and looked like she needed the blanket as much as I did. The pit of my stomach squirmed with discomfort.

"Goblin men," I repeated. It was the catch-all name for both the Fae and the forest creatures. "Yes, I suppose. The Fae."

Mother clutched her chest. "The Fae! What did they do to you?"

I didn't want to explain. I just wanted her to understand. "They took care of me."

"It doesn't look like it," Grandmother quipped.

"I was in trouble, and they found me and did what they could.

I'm better off because of them." My throat closed and eyelids brimmed.

"Ooh!" At the sight of my emotion, Mother drew me into another hug, but this time, her affection didn't comfort me as it had before. I felt cold—bone-cold, as though I wouldn't be warm again.

If it hadn't been mid-morning, I would have asked to go to bed. Perhaps I'd been through enough of an ordeal that they would allow me to retreat to the little room I used to share with Laura. But I was feeling better after those sips of tea. And besides, I couldn't hide from this life. I had to live it. I had to try to heal, even if today I could only manage a tiny, stumbling step.

"Have you been all right?" I asked them.

Another scoff from Grandmother.

Mother hesitated and then said, "No. But we will be now."

I hoped that was true of me too.

❧

I RESTED ALL THAT DAY. OR, AT LEAST, I TRIED TO.

People who had barely spoken to us before now wanted a peek at the miraculous maiden who had returned from the realm of the Fae. Knocking kept coming at the door. Mother was fit to scream at the next gawker or well-wisher or good samaritan who brought food as a ruse to gain entrance to the house. It did feel a little like the house was under siege. This kind of excitement would have made me sparkle with glee before, but now...

The interruptions slowly tapered off. News had spread that I was sleeping, which was false, so they paused their assault until the morning.

I got the feeling that Mother didn't want to make new friends out of previous enemies. Part of me admired her for that. The women in my family were eccentric and poor and disenfranchised, but they were tough.

Night mercifully fell. I heard Mother heave a tremendous sigh in the other room. Despite all the commotion, I hadn't helped at all, hadn't eaten, hadn't left my room. Soon. Soon, I could do all those things.

Soon, I could sleep. Although my body felt exhausted, rest wouldn't truly come. I lay in bed alone, yearning for someone to understand what I'd been through, wondering what was happening back in the castle... I was so full of feelings and thoughts that sleep was impossible.

Hours passed. Restlessness seized me forcefully.

The barrier wasn't far. I could wrap up in layers of socks and jackets and retrieve Laura's gift, if it was still there. Mother and the others deserved it, especially after all they would still endure by having me back in the house—another mouth to feed, neighbors incessantly knocking, and the difficulties that lay ahead of me.

With all these ideas swirling through my mind, I rose, grabbing every piece of warm clothing I could find. There wasn't enough, but I did locate a hat, an extra pair of woolen socks, and gloves that exposed my longest finger. Good enough.

I would go there and back. Laura would want me to.

Unable to leave through the front door—someone was sure to see—I crawled through the window. My knees and elbows protested. I'd aged from a child to an old woman in a few months, it seemed.

The air bit every particle of exposed skin. Huddled and limping, I hurried as fast as I could to the line of trees marking the forest. It was dark, so dark I should have brought a light. No time now. I felt my resolve melting like ice.

Every breath created thick fog that clung to my cheeks and eyelashes.

*Not far...*

If anything was left, I could take it and—

In the distance, hoofbeats sounded. It couldn't be the mare I'd ridden to get here. Surely, she would be long gone by now. It had been hours. Who, then, was riding on the wrong side of the barrier?

My traitorous heart raced. The likeliest person was... I couldn't say his name to myself. The wound of leaving was far too raw. Still, knowledge of him filled my very bones. He was part of me, and I didn't know if I could survive without the pieces he had claimed.

I hurried my pace. Laura's stash of treasure and her note must be close by. I vaguely remembered the area, and knew it had been laid against the barrier itself. That line crossed approximately where I was walking now.

In the blackness, would I even see it? I cursed under my breath. My impulsiveness would be the death of me. *Had* almost been the death of me.

A faint light bobbed into view. My throat closed as I watched it, stunned as a caught kitten. Hiding crossed my mind, but my legs wouldn't obey.

My heart wasn't wrong.

Calyse's big frame trotted into view. As soon as he came close enough for the light to shine on me, he hurdled off his enormous mount and ran so quickly it nearly scared me. He was a supernatural creature and I was a frail human.

His expression was a horrifying mix of fear and anger. The blackness of his pupils had all but engulfed the orange of his eyes. "Lizzie!" he cried as he ran.

I backed up three steps.

Something within him must have sensed the invisible barrier between us because he pulled up short. Fallen pine needles sprayed up. He set down the lantern.

"Lizzie, are you all right?" he demanded, his voice hoarse.

"Yes."

He leaned into the barrier but couldn't pass it. The failed attempt deepened his scowl. "Then where have you been?"

"Lower your voice. You'll scare the village."

"Let them hear!" he bellowed, spreading his arms. "Why did you run away without saying anything?"

"I went home."

He blinked in angry confusion. "All you had to do was ask."

"Do I still have to report all my movements to you?"

With a growl, he snapped, "No. Obviously you don't. But you were in a vulnerable state. When you didn't come back after hours, I thought..." His throat worked. "I thought many, many undesirable things."

In his eyes, I saw wells of pain going back centuries. I had brought that to the surface, just as I suspected I would.

I dropped my gaze. "Well, I'm here. I'm safe."

"You're frozen."

"I was going right back."

"Were you looking for me?"

There it was. The last piece of my heart breaking.

Through the thick pounding of my pulse in my ears, I said, "I was looking for Laura's gift to my family. They never found it."

I resumed my search along the barrier, but slowly. I wasn't sure exactly where it was, and keeping Calyse on the opposite side felt... what? Safer? Safer for my purpose, at least.

"So you were never going to say goodbye?"

My attention snapped back up to his beautiful, dark face. For a moment, I hesitated. "After all you've been through," I finally said, "you deserve peace, Calyse."

His scathing laugh tore open my already bleeding heart. "Peace?"

I glued my eyes to the ground, though I probably would have tripped over the pile of riches if they lay in my path for all the focus I had.

He thrust his hand toward me, cursed, drew it back as if he'd been scalded. "This is peace you're giving me?"

"I'm trying!" I yelled back. If the whole town heard, so be it. "Look at me, Calyse! You know how broken I am. I'm only human, and I might never heal from what happened. You shouldn't have to settle."

"That's my choice," he said, more softly now. "And I choose you. Fuck, I couldn't choose anyone else. I want to take care of you and fight with you. Have you thought about how you gave me a life after *I* was broken?"

A sardonic little laugh—much more bitter than how he usually sounded, warm and friendly—erupted from his lips.

"But this?" He set his jaw. Suddenly, he looked every bit the warrior he was. "Did you ever love me?"

I didn't answer. I couldn't, not because I didn't know the answer, but I knew that voicing it would crumble my resolve to powder.

"Taking the nemesis idea a little far," he said, breaking the silence with a sneer. I heard his pain underneath. Always, that happy demeanor caged in secret emotions he wouldn't let out around any but those he trusted most. I had been one.

"You came up with the name."

He lifted his chin, towering over me even at this little distance. "Did you really think I wouldn't come after you?"

"I didn't know you'd be this angry," I said, letting my pain read like annoyance in my tone.

"I'm furious!" Even as a shout, it sounded like a confession. "You put yourself in danger, left me without a word—"

"Since the moment we met, I've wanted to be free." That part, at least, was true. "I saw my chance, and I had to go, not just for me but for you."

"Free? You don't know me at all if you think I'd prevent you from seeing your family or doing what you like. You're absolutely infuriating, but I love that independent streak. It's not *at odds* with us being together."

Somehow, I had approached the barrier. That invisible line was the only thing separating us.

Calyse leaned forward. For a moment, I thought his strength of both will and body might be enough to break down whatever magic held it in place. He closed his eyes. "Lizzie, I've told you my heart. I'll spill my blood and swear to you again right here. But if you don't love me... if you lied... I'll leave."

I felt every icy breath of wind on my exposed skin. The trees themselves seemed to hold still in anticipation.

Calyse hadn't bothered to put on the leather shirt with its tricky clasp. Instead, he wore a much lighter one that was open at the collar. He must have been freezing too, but if he was, he didn't show it. His proximity warmed my center. All my mind and body gravitated toward him as if we were two magnets. Staying on this side of the barrier became harder and harder. I could comfort him from this terrible pain, but for how long? My addiction hadn't gone away, and I'd almost killed him while possessed with the enemy he'd warned me against.

"Could you..." I could hardly force the words from my mouth. "Could you bring Georgina here tomorrow night so she can meet her son?"

I heard a small, wheezed breath escape from him. He opened his eyes. His look was as full as a conversation. None of that jovial lightness I knew remained. The Calyse of meat hand pies and dirty banter and a quick grin had retreated to the depths.

With a curt, martial nod, he stepped back, putting distance between us. His full mouth formed a hard line.

"Laura placed the gift over there about fifty paces," he said, pointing to my left. "If it's still there."

Without another word, he left.

❧ 28 ❧

Against my wishes, the next morning, both Mother and James accompanied me to see the sheriff. The three of us were tense, not only because I resented James' coming along, but also because I hadn't told Mother about my engagement before I went missing. She took it as a personal affront. I'd only had time to tell Laura before I tasted fairy fruit in the forest.

She wouldn't like my next revelation either. To be more precise, she wouldn't like that I waited to talk about it until the sheriff was there. My news would shake the foundations of Selene—all the maidens still alive could come back. Our little village probably couldn't hold them all. The sheriff needed to know not only because I'd asked Calyse to bring his mother first, but also to help so many people reincorporate themselves into the town.

Honestly, I doubted all of them would come back. Some were so decayed from decades lying asleep that they wouldn't remember their family, and Selene couldn't properly care for all of them. Some had a better chance back in the castle. But even there, most weren't receiving the treatment they needed. I had been the only one with someone to constantly watch over me.

The memories brought a gaping hollow to my chest. Calyse's expression last night, even shrouded in night darkness, burned in my mind. I'd hurt him. Sorrow and fury waged war in the set of his square jaw, the fire of his eyes.

He knew me well enough that he must have understood my reasons. I hadn't run home to Selene because I wanted to leave him, but because I *didn't*. If I hadn't run to a place where he couldn't follow, I would continue to take advantage of his strength and kindness.

For years, he had tried and failed to help Endymion. Watching his friend endure that pain had etched scars into his soul. If I could do anything to prevent a similar experience with me, I would. I did. The decision had cost me my heart. But if I could sacrifice mine so his could be whole, it was worth it.

James set a comforting hand on my shoulder. He'd cleaned himself up from yesterday, even wearing his nicest suit. Still, comparisons between him and Calyse were laughable. James was a nice enough boy to flirt with, but Calyse...

I gave him a wan smile. Soon, I'd have to tell him I couldn't marry him, but I hadn't done it yet. A small part of me feared that I'd have to go through with my promise after all. There was no life for a single woman in Selene.

I raised my fist to knock on the sheriff's door. A small twinge reminded me that Laura and I had planned one day to own this cottage, the best in the village, and grow old like witches together.

James and Mother knocked simultaneously before I made contact. They looked at each other, James surprised, and Mother affronted.

"Hello?" The sheriff answered the door while putting on his

coat. He looked a little like Georgina. He had her eyes. When he saw our little group standing there, his posture relaxed somewhat. "What can I do for you?"

I spoke as quickly as I could. "I need to tell you something."

"Well, come inside. It's cold out there and my wife still has some hash she can heat up."

Two sets of footsteps thundered behind him, no doubt the youngest children. Once they passed, he opened the door wider to let us in. Even as the most enviable dwelling in Selene, it felt cramped with the sheriff and his wife, six children, Mother, James, and me all inside. We navigated past the front room and into the kitchen, which had a large window overlooking the vegetable garden.

"Thank you, sheriff," James said amiably. "I'm glad you're willing to see us. I've asked what Lizzie has to say, but I'm afraid she won't tell me."

"It was more important that I tell you," I replied acidly, turning from James to the older man.

"What is it?" He looked genuinely curious as he found a seat at the dining room table, a huge, misshapen thing that must have been an heirloom. It looked like a cross-section of an enormous tree. Everything here reminded me of Laura, of the life I wanted to live in the Fae kingdom.

"The women who went missing," I began.

"Please, sit." He gestured with a rough hand to the seat adjacent to his.

"I'd rather stand."

"You're half-dead. Take the seat," Mother instructed quietly.

"I'd rather stand." At that point, it was just stubbornness, and I knew it. I had—how had Calyse put it?—an independent streak. It got me into trouble more often than it helped, but I clung to the shred of autonomy it provided.

The sheriff's wife entered the kitchen, blinked to see our group there, and promptly set to work serving us.

"Did you ever have anyone go missing?" I asked her.

She seemed surprised that I addressed her. "Yes." Her voice was soft, almost apologetic. I felt the confines of this little town squeeze my insides tighter. "A school friend, my aunt..."

"We've all had people go missing," the sheriff prompted me.

"Your mother, for example."

His demeanor darkened at the memory. "Yes. My mother."

"What I'm here to say is that I've met other women who disappeared. Many of them are still alive, including your mother. And she's coming here."

Everyone started talking at once. Questions, exclamations— even the two oldest children, who had been listening from around the corner, stepped forward to express their shock.

"I don't know how many of them will be able to come back," I said over the din, wishing I'd taken the chair. "Some of us are... not doing well. I don't remember all their names, so I can't answer for everyone, but a good number of us were put into an enchanted sleep."

Mother's expression of surprise turned skeptical, the layers of protection around her heart hardening again. I saw it there—she doubted my word.

"I'm telling the truth," I said. "I've asked— I know that the sheriff's mother is coming to see him tonight. Georgina. We spoke together about how much she misses you." I held the sheriff's stare.

"Where?" he asked brusquely. "When?" His was the professional version of what I observed in Mother.

"The forest. Tonight." I hadn't requested a specific time, I realized. Calyse would probably bring Georgina to reunite with her son sooner rather than later. My breathing grew shallow. If I knew him, he'd be ready as soon as the sun went down.

"Alone?"

A chill swept down my back. What could I say? How much of my story was I ready to tell?

"She'll have... protection," I said.

"What?" Mother asked, incredulous. "Fae?"

"Fae?" James, who had been struck dumb by my news, found his voice again. "You met the Fae?" He drew closer to me as though relieved that I hadn't fully fallen prey to either their famous violence or seductions. "My brave girl," he whispered, though I was sure Mother could hear. It was terribly embarrassing.

"They're actually..." But what they were, actually, I couldn't think. I couldn't speak for Endymion or the others, but one Fae was great and kind and exciting.

"Is she going to have a member of the Fae with her?" the sheriff asked. His eyes shone with a mixture of curiosity, hope, and suspicion.

I'd grown up with the stories, same as he had. The Fae were wild, untamable beings who left our young men corpses and our women ravished. If I told the truth, would they threaten Calyse? I doubted they could hurt him, unless in some kind of coordinated ambush, but the very idea made my blood hot.

"Yes," I said, more loudly than I meant to. "He'll take good care of her. He took good care of me."

From the corner of my eye, I saw Mother's jaw tighten in silent disagreement. She didn't know how much thinner and weaker and *worse* I'd been after just waking up.

"You saw a Fae?" This time it was the sheriff's daughter. She wore her hair in a braid like mine. Her blue eyes were perfectly round.

"Now, let them be. It doesn't do to dwell on goblin men," said the sheriff's wife quietly, ushering the children out.

I drew myself up. I knew I'd encounter this mix of attitudes. In this village, only I knew the truth, so only I could stand up for Calyse. "This one will keep your mother safe," I told the sheriff. "I've never known someone so selfless and so helpful. I wouldn't have made it back without him."

"Will this... Fae bring the others as well?" the sheriff asked carefully.

"If I ask him to." My heart twisted. I didn't want to ask him to do anything else. If I had to, I could go to the castle myself and fetch the women. I just had to sit down first...

Why was I so stubborn? People wanted to help me in small ways and I bristled at their attempts. Just because no one in the village was addicted to fairy fruit didn't mean they couldn't care about me.

"And... Laura?" Mother asked.

Since my arrival, I'd excused myself from the flurry of attention as much as possible, which hadn't given me time to explain everything. "She's..." I laughed a little at the beautiful absurdity of it. "She's Queen of the Fae. She married the Fae King Endymion. He takes care of her." I could feel their protests bubbling like a pot about to overflow. "She loves him." I locked eyes with Mother to show her how serious I was.

"Queen of the Fae?" James repeated. "Lizzie, I love your stories, but—"

"Laura's the one with the stories," I said sharply. "Every word I've said here is true. I know I sounds crazy."

The sheriff looked up at where Mother stood beside me. "If it's all right with you, I would like Lizzie to show me where this Fae is going to bring my mother tonight. If she's lying, she's lying. Or—I'm sorry—maybe she's just been wandering in the forest too long. Anyone could get a bit of forest madness after that."

Mother chewed the inside of her cheek. Her eyes darted to James.

"I can go," he assured her.

I bit my tongue. I had to tell that boy today that he needn't be by my side. I wouldn't marry him. Even if singlehood made me a pariah or a witch, I'd risk it.

"I'll be there as well," the sheriff said politely.

Happily, no one asked the obvious question about how I'd arranged all this. Already, I'd been back to the woods alone.

"Shall we meet here at sundown?" I said.

A few more minutes of pleasantries finally saw the three of us back on our way. The sheriff was a decent sort of person. I was glad for Georgina. But I was too tired for small talk.

When we reached the door of our cottage, I yearned for a couple hours' rest, but I turned to Mother instead. "You go ahead," I said. "I need to talk to James."

A boyish smile spread across his face.

Mother squinted meaningfully at him. He was to behave or she'd find out about it. "Don't be too long. We've added extra logs to keep the fire hotter."

Laura's gifts, the lost women... The castle held more and more to go back for, even if I was going to stay in Selene for good. I felt wrapped in its tethers.

With Mother inside, I turned my focus to James. He was attractive, in a simple kind of way. Light brown hair, freckles, deep-set eyes. I wasn't surprised I'd snogged him a few times at the barn and, before that, the bakery.

"James," I began.

"We don't have to rush things," he said quickly. "I know you must have been through so much. As soon as you're better, we can plan the wedding. You can take a couple weeks if you want to."

He was so earnest, I actually smiled. "No, James. I... I can't marry you anymore."

His brows lowered. "I can wait a little while while you're—"

"James."

He stuttered to a halt.

"Thank you for the help you've given me since I came back." It had consisted mainly of intense looks of concern, but that was still more than nothing. "But I don't love you."

His lowered eyebrows twitched. "I can take care of you. The bakery does well and you've been through a lot. I can wait."

"I don't want to wait. I'm calling off the engagement. Thank you for everything."

His look of confusion turned upset. "You promised me, Lizzie."

I sighed, regretful. "I said yes when I thought I didn't have a choice. You'll make a good husband someday, but not to me."

"You won't be beautiful forever."

I was almost glad he'd said it. It made my break from him taste sweet rather than bitter. "Then I'll hide away in a cottage somewhere with my cats and birds."

"Crazy girl," he said affectionately. In his tone, I heard more than a little disappointment.

But I didn't need him to take care of me. I didn't need anyone.

I just desperately, desperately wanted someone who understood me to care for me.

I wanted Calyse.

I always knew I liked Grandmother. She wouldn't put up with anyone's bullshit, and she was the only one brave enough to accompany me into the forest. Of course, the sheriff was there too, but Mother still insisted I bring someone else along if James wouldn't go.

After I'd called off the engagement, James left. I had a feeling that the rumors about the crazy women at the edge of the village would only grow louder. My sudden return from the Other Kingdom had no doubt already done that. Choosing singleness over marriage to an eligible young bachelor wouldn't improve my reputation either.

Grandmother grouched about the cold weather more constantly than usual. She was nervous. Among her grumblings, I heard the name of some of her school friends who had disappeared. I walked close to her. This was my third time entering the forest, so I knew more about what to expect. If I wasn't terrified, then she could take comfort too.

No, terrified wasn't the right word. In fact, walking into the woods felt almost like going home.

A home that wasn't mine anymore.

Snuggling my chin into the new scarf a well-wisher had knitted me, I forged onward. Next to us, the sheriff carried a lantern aloft. His wide eyes betrayed his anticipation as I led the little group to the edge of the barrier. At least, the edge as I remembered it. That was the thing about an invisible barrier—it could be hard to sense where it was.

Surrounded by fir trees now, I stopped. No lilting music from a party of forest creatures. No clop of hooves. Even the birds fell silent. But I dimly recognized a thin, broken stump from the night before. This was the spot where I had seen Calyse.

"He should meet us here," I said, throat dry. How long would we have to wait?

Grandmother and the sheriff peered into the blackness of night as if some creature would rear up. Actually, that wasn't impossible. Most of the snow had melted or been disturbed. Only thin patches of it remained in the shadiest spots, like gray puddles sparkling in the moonlight. The air still smelled of snow, though, sharp and fresh.

My breathing grew shallow. Nerves bundled together in my belly and I looked to Grandmother to ground myself.

The three of us listened, like beasts of the forest ourselves, breath puffing into the air like tiny gusts of smoke.

After a couple minutes, the sheriff looked at me. "Are you sure this is the place? I don't want to keep you two out in the cold."

"We're fine!" Grandmother snapped.

Perhaps that was where I'd gotten that independent streak.

"They'll come," I assured him. I'd bet my life on it. Calyse wasn't one to go back on his word. Anyone who could keep a secret for centuries could be trusted with this one task.

"I can wait here alone," the sheriff said.

"No." It was true that he could, but I wanted to be here too.

Organizing the meeting between lost loved ones gave me purpose. And Calyse was coming.

"Shh!" Grandmother hissed.

We all went silent.

I heard the faint swish of pine needles moments before two huge horses came into view. The Fae were always quieter than I expected.

In the dim glow of the lantern, an enormous black horse stepped forward. On it sat Laura with Endymion, clad in full black and gold royal regalia. A white horse strode beside them bearing Georgina and Calyse.

All four dismounted to come closer. I wasn't breathing.

"Laura girl!" Grandmother exclaimed, rushing past the barrier to embrace her granddaughter. I admired her bravery. Endymion looked fierce, taller than any man in the village. He was strong, with a cruel, sensuous curve of his lip.

Laura met her hug and held her. My eyes stung to watch them. Why couldn't the others be here for this reunion too? I'd convince them to come later, with Grandmother's testimony to back me up.

Endymion merely observed everyone like the Fae King he was. I knew, though, that beneath his insolence, he loved my sister more than life.

I finally looked at Calyse. He wasn't looking at me. In fact, he was pointedly *not* looking at me. Instead, he urged Georgina forward.

Thanks to Endymion's magic, mother and son looked the same age. Georgina had barely aged at all during her years of enchanted sleep. Slowly, still clad in the simple white dress we'd all worn, she approached the sheriff. "Gabriel?" she asked uncertainly.

The sheriff stepped forward haltingly, as if he thought the

barrier might stop him from approaching. "Yes."

"My Gabriel?" Her hoarse voice came out a whisper.

He set down the lantern. Steam from his mouth came out in quicker bursts.

Georgina looked like a ghost, pale in the darkness.

"Are you... Georgina?" the sheriff asked, each word quiet and labored. This was outside of his experience. "Are you my mother?"

Georgina's lip trembled and her fingers reached forward just a little. Perhaps she was a ghost, incapable of touching the living. But then the sheriff reached out too and took her hand. They looked at their joined hands with confusion and wonder and joy. Emotion contorted the sheriff's face as he grappled with the truth of this miracle.

My chest ached with the beauty and sorrow of so many lost years now restored. When the mother and son began talking low to one another—asking questions, proclaiming their love, how they'd missed each other—my attention flicked once more to the warrior Fae in the shadows.

Grim satisfaction but no joy crossed his rugged features. He still wasn't looking at me.

I realized I was the only one who hadn't crossed the barrier. Everyone else stood on the other side, and I remained on the threshold of the human world alone. It felt like the breathless wait before a plunge.

If I chose to jump.

I picked my way along the barrier's edge until I stood across from him. Finally, his eyes met mine. The pain in them nearly stole my breath.

"Thank you for bringing them here," I said. I hadn't expected to see Laura, but that was a welcome surprise. She had probably worried about me too.

Calyse stood too far away for me to speak quietly. "If you want to talk to me," he said, "don't stand on the wrong side of the bloody barrier."

I licked my cold lips. "I do want to talk." What I would say, I still didn't know. Laura was the planner. I simply acted. And this time, I doubted that I'd chosen the best thing.

"Then come here."

I didn't move. Something would change if I crossed this threshold. Was I ready to face it?

Calyse stood impassive, waiting.

After a few fortifying breaths, I stepped forward. And again. The barrier was behind me. Calyse was ahead. Heart pounding, I approached him until we were face to face.

"That's better," he said. This time he was back in his dark leathers. A band tied up his hair. "Now, what did you want to say?"

His expression was a careful neutral. I missed his smile, his smolder—anything but this wall erected to protect him from more devastating hurt.

Behind me came the tearful murmurs of reunion. "Calyse," I began, unsure, "I want you to be happy." An unexpected sob choked me.

His shoulders tensed. Frown deepening, he just said, "What about you?"

"What *about* me?"

"Are you happy?"

The question was so simple. "Calyse, I... I'm selfish. I'm trouble."

The first hint of a smile thawed his lips. "Damn right you are." That wicked look. I could have kissed him right there, lost myself in him.

"You'll be happier without me," I soldiered on before I could lose my nerve. "Maybe not right away, but you will. I'm not doing this because I don't love you but... because I do."

He sidled closer, still not touching. His dark face above me furrowed with compassion. "Love isn't only happiness." His voice had lowered so much I felt the rumble in my core. "Sometimes it's holding each other up. Sometimes it hurts so much you want to die. But what is life without love?"

His question echoed my own so closely that again I wondered if he knew my thoughts. A tiny, glowing hope bloomed again in my chest, afraid to shine.

"Let me hold you up."

A hard lump in my throat prevented my response until I could finally talk around it. "I'm still human, though. I'll grow old and you'll stay gorgeous like this. It can't work."

He slowly, gently took my hands in his, threading our fingers together. "We'll make it work. Your sister is one of us. We'll figure out something."

Laura had gained her amber eyes and powers only after Endymion had been killed. Part of her life had been given in exchange for his. I shuddered to consider how awful that must have been.

"It's too hard," I said.

"That's something I would say, but not about this."

"Calyse!" Despite everything, I found myself smiling.

His next words were slow, insistent. "Let me hold you up."

He loved me despite my craving for fairy fruit, my wildness, my surly attitude, my abandonment of him. I wanted what he offered so much I nearly felt sick, but could I take it? Was it right?

Calyse deserved the world, but what he wanted was me.

"I won't be perfect," I warned.

"I will be, so at least that's one of us," he teased.

I held his fingers tighter. His scent was making me light-headed. "I can't promise that I won't do stupid things like going after fairy fruit."

"I will expect stupid things, as long as you always come back to me." He bent down so his forehead touched mine. I soaked in the warmth of his skin, the nearness of his breath. "I won't always be happy, and sometimes I'll play the flute in the middle of the night."

"Just for me?" I breathed.

"Of course."

"Naked?"

He made a deep growling noise. "Even better." His hands snaked around my waist, the hard muscles of his arms pressing against my sides. "Do you love me?"

"Yes. Do you love me?"

"Always. So we have enough. You don't have to run anymore."

I swallowed hard.

"Don't act like you're not worthy of love, Lizzie. None of us are," he went on. He snuggled his face into the crook of my neck. "I've killed and stolen and lied in my lifetime. And I've done filthy things with a human woman."

When a small chuckle escaped my throat, he nipped at it as if he could feed on the sound.

"Come back with me."

I felt every movement of his full lips against my neck as he spoke the words.

"I want to help the women who want to return to Selene," I murmured.

"Then do it."

"And I want to visit."

"I hope so. Bring me human things. You've been no help teaching me about other cultures."

My heart felt close to bursting. Was it selfish to have done so much wrong and yet feel so happy?

"I'm sorry," I said. "I'm sorry for everything."

Faint light glimmered over the area where the two of us stood entwined in the dark. The sheriff must have picked up the lantern again. I hadn't considered that anyone might be watching us. The others had been so enraptured by their own reunions.

I stepped back from Calyse and turned.

Laura's expression was utterly knowing. Grandmother looked horrified, the sheriff confused. Georgina never looked away from her son.

Endymion's lips curved in a smirk.

❧ 30 ❧

A few days later, I wrote down the woman's name and the family members she could remember from Selene. Although I'd asked many of them questions in my search for the bird woman with black eyes, I hadn't properly memorized their names. How I missed this woman, I wasn't sure.

It was Jeanie, Grandmother's friend who had gone missing in their youth. She looked about forty now, but that was just because of the preservation that enchanted sleep provided. Her round face and expressive gestures were a testament to how lively she'd been. The same haze settled over her as it did over the rest of them—us—but she was starting to break through the surface of it as I had.

Grandmother would be thrilled to know Jeanie was still alive. In four days, I planned to travel back to the village with a small group of women to reunite them with their families. Before I left, Grandmother had assured me she would try to get Mother and Grandmother to go into the woods to see Laura for themselves. I hoped she would succeed.

A touch on my shoulder made me turn around.

Laura stood behind me, wearing a green silk gown with wide cutouts in the bodice.

"Thank you," I told Jeanie before giving my sister me full attention. "You look conspiratorial today."

"Conspiratorial?" She laughed. "No, but I do have a gift for you."

I set the pen and paper on the long dining table where I'd found the cursed fairy fruit. Apart from a few ruby smudges, no evidence remained of the pile of pomegranate seeds. My mouth watered for them still, but my craving was merely an ache, a tug, rather than blinding desperation. Perhaps eventually I would barely hear its call.

Laura held her hands behind her back. It wasn't an occasion for gifts—at least, I didn't think so. I was still getting my bearings in terms of what day it was. "What is it?"

She held out a bound sheaf of black paper with golden writing on it. It didn't have a proper cover as the bookbinder would have included, but the creamy darkness of it with Laura's familiar handwriting made me burn with curiosity. I took it.

"It's a new story," she explained.

I beamed. It had been ages since I read one of Laura's stories. The book I'd given her for her birthday had apparently disappeared. "Oh, Laura! Orlando and Genevieve?"

"Not this time. You'll have to read it and see."

THAT WAS HOW CALYSE FOUND ME: READING LAURA'S BOOK AS I lay on my stomach in bed. It told the story of two sisters, differently named but obviously us, finding love and adventure deep in the forest. The Lizzie character saved the Laura character on multiple occasions. I came out looking like the hero, and she also wrote me a passionate love affair with a handsome prince.

"What's that?" he asked, slinging off his knife belt before sitting on the edge of his bed next to me.

I rolled to the side to look at him. This book was a treat, this bed was a treat, and so was this life I had with Calyse. Warmth surged through me, and I smiled at him.

He raised his black eyebrows. "That good?"

"Right now?" I answered. "That good."

"No more running away?"

"Mmmm..." I pretended to muse, sitting up, hip to hip, next to him. His solid, masculine presence comforted me, made me want more. I thought I could stay here with him forever. "Probably not."

"Probably?" he repeated low in his throat, eyeing me with a mischievous twinkle.

"I need more convincing."

"Or punishment, you crazy human girl."

My stomach jolted as desire pulsed at my core. "That could do it."

He hummed, a naughty sound, and cupped my face. "What am I going to do with you?"

"Terribly dirty things, I hope." I reached around and undid the now-familiar clasp at the nape of his neck to loosen his molded leather top. Looking into his fiery eyes, I felt my insides go molten.

He spoke so close to my mouth that I felt his lips against mine. "I have a great capability for dirty things."

"Then what are you waiting for?"

He tasted my lips and then pulled away. I tried to follow, but the hand that had cupped my cheek now held my braid, preventing me from getting any closer. Frustrated, I stared a challenge at him. He stared back with a smirk. "Now, now," he said, "you haven't been punished yet."

I cocked my jaw, amused and expectant. "Well then?"

"Lie down," he commanded. "Take off your dress."

I missed the heat from his body when he stood and strode to the other side of the room to light a candle.

Between his sure hands and the burning sensation of the wax, my pleasure mounted quickly. Always, he watched to see that I was enjoying his painful teasing. "Naughty girl," he murmured as he let a drop fall near my nipple. I sucked in a gasp. His breaths, I heard, were growing shallower. He soothed each burn with kisses and rough strokes of his thumb. The most painful part was waiting for him to touch me where I needed. For long minutes, he only touched me briefly, with no pressure, to feel how wet I'd grown for him. He growled his approval, pinching and burning me until I trembled.

Only then, when I'd grown wild, did he give me what I asked for. He pumped in, hard and deep and possessive, before leaning over me close enough that I could feel the firm ridges of his muscled torso as he undulated against me. I came apart with a scream.

Out of breath, we parted with sloppy kisses. After a comfortable quiet filled only with our panting as we lay side by side, I said, "Am I forgiven, then?"

He tipped his generous, bruised mouth. "Probably. I might have to do that again."

"Sleep short," I quipped.

He grinned, caressing my bare arm. "Sleep short," he agreed.

# THANK YOU!

Thank you for reading *Trapped by the Fae*! Please consider leaving a review. Reviews help authors like me get found by more readers.

Now, read on for a sneak peek of another story that will leave you begging for more...

Or, read *Wings and Blindness*—a story that asks what if Psyche were sent to kill Eros but things heated up—now, for free if you sign up for my newsletter!

READ A SNEAK PEEK OF ZORA FOX'S NEXT
DEATHLESS LOVE NOVEL, *FLOWERS AND THE FAR
REALM*!

*What if Persephone could bring spirits back from the dead?*

Without even counting his unruly shadow self, overworked Hades can't keep up with the incoming corpses, monsters, and misfits sent to the infamous Far Realm. His desire to give everyone another chance at life—or afterlife—has become almost impossible. Without help, that is.

Seph dreams of romance and adventure while she works in the royal garden under her mother's watchful eye. When her ability to bring plants to life catches Hades' attention, he ignores her protests and steals her away to his kingdom.

Although other gods fear Hades with all his intensity, elegance, and mysterious power, Seph (or Persephone as he insists on calling her) can't help but be lured in. But Hades can't allow their fiery connection to ignite. The Far Realm needs him focused, and innocent Seph might not survive the darkness that lurks beneath his own skin.

The little goddess emerged from behind the square of hedges. Her eyes were huge, blue in a bronze face. Her yellow dress accentuated the smoothness of her skin with a belt cinching in the curve of her waist. The top part of the dress dipped down to show off her collarbone and a dark shadow of cleavage. Her powerful fingers remained mobile at her sides.

It was difficult to see from here, but this girl's power was reviving dead flowers. As I stared, I only caught her doing it once. A brown petal turned white just before we made eye contact.

She looked afraid. Made sense. It was rare for me to find a substantially different reaction from anyone meeting me for the first time.

I stepped back to assess her as she topped the shallow flight of stairs. Her chest trembled with shaky breathing. She looked extremely young, twenties maybe. Hopefully I hadn't come on a fool's errand. The Far Realm couldn't spare me.

"I have no further need of you," I told the human queen. Whether she was insulted, I didn't know, because I didn't watch her go.

I clasped my hands behind my back. "Persephone?"

"Seph."

I arched a brow.

"I prefer Seph, and everybody calls me that. But Persephone's fine too." She swallowed, her full mouth pursing as she did.

"What is your power, Seph?" I didn't like the nickname as much as her full name.

"I tend the plants in the palace garden here."

"That's your job. What is your power?" The information I'd gotten in Zenia had better be right. A minor goddess who had the power of life, the censor had said. The longer I looked at Persephone—Seph—the more I doubted she would last long in the Far

Realm. It smelled tame here, floral. All these soft edges stirred something inside me I didn't like.

"I can revive flowers by touching them," she answered.

"Just flowers?"

"Other plants too. And insects." She looked almost ashamed at that.

"And," I prompted, sensing there was more.

"I can make new flowers grow too. I feel them in the earth and I just—"

"What about animals, people?"

"What?"

"Can you revive them?"

She cast a glance to the side, almost as if she were looking for someone, but we were completely alone.

"I've never tried," she finally answered.

My brows ticked down. She had the ability to revive living things and she'd *never tried?* I was wasting my time here. This girl was too young, too naïve, for what I wanted her to do.

It was time to go.

I got halfway across the flagstones before I halted and whirled back. Her dress did a pretty little thing as she twirled to meet my gaze again. Despite her ignorance of the harsher realities of life, she was alarmingly cute. Beautiful, even.

It was just that godsdamned ascension ceremony getting into my head. I hadn't taken time to unwind.

"Then it's time to try now," I said curtly, marching back to her. This was too important to abandon so quickly.

This time, I stood closer to her, close enough to smell the faint scent of strawberries wafting off her hair. Inside, the thing I kept leashed began to stir with excitement. Curling my lip in impatience, I held out my hand and sliced a line across the palm.

It was always a good idea to keep a knife handy. You never knew when you'd need it.

Persephone gasped and covered her mouth. Her eyes flashed from my face to my bloody hand and back.

"Fix it," I ordered calmly.

"I don't know if I can—"

"Fix. It."

Her hands shook as she raised them, a concentrating line forming between her brows. "I... Normally, I have to touch the... the plants I'm healing. Is that all right?"

I almost smiled. I hadn't encountered innocence this profound in years. "Fine."

Her touch was soft, exploratory. Small fingers moved gently over the skin of my palm, avoiding the welling blood. It was careful, whatever she was doing. I found myself enthralled with the designs she drew on me, feeling for... something. I didn't know how this kind of power worked, which is why I needed someone like her. If she could pass this test.

The pressure under her fingertips increased, and she closed her eyes. As though she didn't fully realize what she was doing, she brought her other hand up to cradle my calloused one so she could push down harder. Now she didn't avoid the blood anymore. She made spirals with it, new lines, and then she stroked the wound itself.

For the first time, the cut stung. When she made contact with it, my body reacted more strongly than it should have. My hand pulsed and danced with pinpricks. She rubbed the wound, almost petting it, her movements sensual and precise. She'd figured something out.

With one last stroke down the center, she exhaled and opened her eyes. The hand that hadn't been tracing my cut pulled away as if she'd been caught doing something wrong. My blood glazed her fingertips.

I wiped the thumb of my uninjured hand across my bloody palm. Under the red was smooth skin.

When we locked eyes again, hers were bright and uncertain. The hint of a smile played on her lips, though. Victory, it said. Pride.

I raised one side of my mouth in return. We were both breathing harder than we should have been. But this, *this*, could change everything.

READ THE REST OF *FLOWERS AND THE FAR REALM* NOW!

# READ MORE BY ZORA FOX

Fae and Shadow duology
    *End of the Forest*
    *Trapped by the Fae*

Deathless Love—novels
    *Wings and Blindness*
    *Flowers and the Far Realm*
    *Flame and Warpaint*
    *Temptation and Tridents*

Deathless Love—novellas
    *Storm and Sanctuary*
    *Full Moons and Vampires*
    *Candle Wax and Sunlight*

Deathless Love—short stories
    *Lovers and Monsters*
    *Secrets and Midnights*